Praise for

"[An] auspicious debut . . . a good, solid read."
—Steve Perry

"The action is nonstop and deadly, the
details compelling,
the story surefooted and satisfying."
—Rutledge Etheridge, author of *The First Duelist*

Laicy Campbell came to earth to learn the way of the sword . . . and the way of the Zen masters. Her training had been rigorous and thorough, and she became a ronin, traveling the colonies in search of danger and enlightenment. Nothing guided her but the calling.

She had only planned on staying on the arid, dying planet of Rune for a few days. But it was there, in the brutal deserts that she at last discovered the task she was meant for, the temple that must be rebuilt. And the shadow warrior who would lead her to her ultimate destination as a searcher and a samurai. She would be called IROSHI . . .

Don't miss

## *The Glaive*

second in the gripping series featuring the warrior Iroshi

*Ace Books by* Cary Osborne

IROSHI
THE GLAIVE
PERSEA

# CARY OSBORNE

ACE BOOKS, NEW YORK

If you purchased this book without a cover, you should be aware that this book is stolen property. It was reported as "unsold and destroyed" to the publisher, and neither the author nor the publisher has received any payment for this "stripped book."

This book is an Ace original edition,
and has never been previously published.

PERSEA

An Ace Book / published by arrangement with
the author

PRINTING HISTORY
Ace edition / December 1996

All rights reserved.
Copyright © 1996 by Cary Osborne.
Cover art by Jean-Francois Podevin.
This book may not be reproduced in whole or in part,
by mimeograph or any other means, without permission.
For information address: The Berkley Publishing Group,
200 Madison Avenue, New York, NY 10016.

The Putnam Berkley World Wide Web site address is
http://www.berkley.com/berkley

Make sure to check out PB Plug, the science
fiction/fantasy newsletter, at http://www.pbplug.com

ISBN: 0-441-00397-4

ACE®
Ace Books are published by the Berkley Publishing Group,
200 Madison Avenue, New York, NY 10016.
ACE and the "A" design are trademarks
belonging to Charter Communications, Inc.

PRINTED IN THE UNITED STATES OF AMERICA

10 9 8 7 6 5 4 3 2 1

# 1

The racer settled down with a final, gentle shudder. Iroshi gave her own shudder. No matter how many times she visited Rune-Nelson, nothing prevented that initial reaction. Being stranded for a week all those years ago was enough to give anyone nightmares. Even her second visit, five years later, when she had returned to bring back the booreecki, had restarted those nightmares. Arthur and Guinevere, the breeding pair of carnivores she had raised from pups, were long dead, the breed's life span being only fifteen years on average. Their legacy was the telepathic relationship between their descendants and the Glaive members working here. At times it became almost a symbiosis.

But that adventure had happened decades ago. Living in the past was becoming a very bad habit, one that she was not really old enough, at eighty-seven, to start practicing.

*Agreed!* Ensi's familiar voice said inside her head.

She smiled. He had been her constant companion for over sixty years, and he had changed so little. Of course, those sixty years were a very small part of his total existence. What did it feel like to be hundreds of years old? Not that she didn't feel that old right now.

The crew must be about ready to open the outer hatches. Iroshi pushed herself out of the chair, and her elbow cracked. She rubbed it a moment, then straightened her grey tunic. The hem of the matching skirt swished against the ankles of her boots when she took the first steps toward the cabin door, opened it, and stepped out.

Harleq, her steward, waited just outside. He straightened the collar of her tunic and nodded his satisfaction. As soon as she left the racer, he would make his way to her quarters in the university and unpack what she would need for the next few days.

Scanlon waited at the other end of the hall, immaculate in his own maroon uniform and grey boots. The color was good for him as it was for everyone, it seemed. Especially with his dark brown hair that he kept short. It was difficult to say when maroon had become the choice for formal occasions. However, this was definitely a formal occasion, and one that filled her with unease, if not outright dread. One reason she had chosen to wear grey, so as not to make too much of this visit. A contradiction, but one that would keep others off balance.

Scanlon, Glaive Marshal, turned his head, saw her, and smiled. His stance was confident, the expression in his blue eyes nearly bold. He looked like the—what term had Crowell used?—the "heir apparent." It had stuck even though the words smacked of monarchy. Besides, there were still several candidates for replacing her as leader of the Glaive after she died. Chances were that she would live another thirty or forty years, but it was good to have someone standing in the wings, trained to assume leadership, familiar with events and policies....

*And who espouses all of your policies,* Ensi finished.

"Yes," she said silently. "At least, someone who believes that 'Iroshi' is a person, not a title."

Scanlon stepped back a little to make sure she could get ahead of him. She nodded and led the way toward the main hatch. Most of the crew lined the short route. Captain Jarys waited at the ramp. She had been captain of the racer ever since Ferguson, the original captain, retired. He, too, was dead now.

"Everyone is gathered outside," the captain announced.

Iroshi nodded and stepped into sunlight.

A cheer rose in the midday air, and she acknowledged the greeting with a nod. Martin Dukane, commander of this outpost, waited at the foot of the ramp, ready to welcome with official greetings and false innocence. As expected, he wore the maroon uniform, which set off his tanned face and auburn hair handsomely.

*Do not judge his motives too quickly,* Ensi warned. *It is still possible that his actions are not what they seem, or that his motives are less self-serving.*

Iroshi started down the ramp.

"You're the one who told me what he's up to, Ensi. Are you having second thoughts?"

*Possibly doubts about my own objectivity.*

Dukane, all six-foot-seven of him, held out his left hand and she took it in her own, letting go when her feet were firmly set on the tarmac. She needed no assistance in moving from one place to another, and would not have it appear as if she did. Nor would she have it appear that she and Dukane were overly close.

Glancing sideways at her escort, Iroshi said, "I thought I said no ceremonies." It might be a formal visit, but she had ordered that the reception be kept simple.

"I couldn't disappoint all of these people," Dukane said. "It isn't often that Iroshi visits us."

Now here was someone who used "Iroshi" like a title. Scanlon cleared his throat behind her, and she barely hid her scowl. Scanlon knew how she detested hearing the name used in that way. She would not become the new Caesar, and he might be the one to prevent that happening in the next generation of the Glaive.

The path led between two rows of Glaive members toward a pavilion erected at the edge of the tarmac. Red, green, and yellow banners cracked in the warm wind, all bearing a representation of the original temple, symbol of their guild. In the distance, the well-remembered forest stood—relatively untouched, if those orders had been followed more closely than the ones regarding the reception. Man's newest intrusion on the world would leave as few permanent marks as possible. Even the ancient ruins had been rebuilt, until such necessities, such as this landing field, were built. It had been particularly pleasing to be told that this hill site, with its topmost building nearly intact, had proved most malleable to the Glaive's needs.

She climbed the four steps to the pavilion platform and took the chair Dukane indicated. Scanlon sat to her left while their host moved to stand behind a small podium. The Glaive members gathered in front, standing, while in the distance, the racer's crew of five watched from the two main hatches. It was possible to see Captain Jarys smiling, or was that her imagination? The captain had certainly heard her ranting about such ceremonies enough times to know her mind. To one side, other civilians watched, looking like outsiders because of the distance between their gathering and the members. Here, there was a greater sense of their being outsiders than on Rune-Nevas. That situation would have to be changed.

"It is with extreme pleasure that we welcome Iroshi to Rune-Nelson," Dukane announced into the renewed quiet. Even the wind had dropped, and the banners only waved slightly. "Although her visit will be short, the honor is great and will be long remembered."

Smiles expanded on several faces in the crowd. Just looking over those faces would make anyone believe this was the hotbed of Iroshi worship. Dukane's voice groaned into the background as she studied the looks, the postures of this group. The longer she looked at them, however, the stronger became the sense of delineation. Not only were the civilians separated from the members, the members themselves were divided into two groups, standing side by side, yet separated physically and mentally.

To the left, human hosts with human companions. To the right, human hosts with Nevan companions. It was the former group that had the most beautiful, adoring smiles.

*You were right,* Ensi said. *Human spirits may not be old enough for bonding. A human with a human ... Too many of the old yearnings still exist.*

"True," she answered silently. "Perhaps only a few can make the transition. This is going to cause numerous problems no matter what we decide to do."

Dukane's voice changed, indicating that he was nearing the end of his speech.

"We need to make a decision soon, she continued." "I still think letting the spirits age would be best."

*Like a fine wine.*

"I suppose. They definitely need more time, a greater distance from their former lives."

Dukane turned toward her, his smile increasing her uneasy feelings. For the moment, it was time to tell everyone how much she appreciated the welcome, and what a good job all of them had been doing.

*An urgent message.*

Iroshi looked up from the computer display. After two hours studying reports on excavations and epigraphy, an interruption was welcome. Except, urgent meant trouble.

"What is it?"

*There are problems with the project on Djed. Erik Greer and Garon need to talk to you.*

"All right."

Silence; then another familiar voice spoke inside her head.

*Good morning, Iroshi,* Garon said. *I am afraid that our scientist friends are not being totally honest with us, even though it was they who asked for Glaive help.*

"The new formula isn't what they described?"

*Yes, it seems that it is. Prolonging life was their original project, but they may have stumbled onto something else: a means of preserving the spirit after death. They call it persea, by the way. It's ancient Egyptian, meaning "the point from which the sun rises," or so they say. It may be they hope to bring people back from death or even to transfer spirits into other bodies. Like we do in the Glaive.*

# 2

"I don't understand," Dukane exclaimed. "Why must you remove me from my post?"

He looked as if he was about to leap from his chair. His overlarge sword was propped against the arm of his chair in its scabbard. From across the desk, Iroshi watched closely. His large, muscular body was tensed, whether for fight or flight she could not tell because his shield was in place. This was a delicate moment, one that must not be mishandled. However, no matter what she said or did, Dukane was bound to be disappointed. At the same time, she must get this task completed here on Rune-Nelson before moving on to the problems on Djed.

"This is not a punishment, nor is it meant to indicate that the work you've done here was not good," she said. "It is simply time for you to move on. Few Glaive members have permanent assignments."

"But nothing is finished. To leave everything that I have begun and never see the finish—the translation of the runes, exploration of the planet, researching the technology left behind." He took a deep breath. "We proved that the people who lived here were related to those from Rune-Nevas. Does this mean nothing?"

"It means a lot . . ." she began.

"And the booreecki? The work we've done with them: bringing them from the brink of extinction; training them to limit their telepathic powers so as not to disturb people; and we've come so far with training them as companions to Glaive members."

"We know this is difficult, but you have been here fifteen years. It is time to renew yourself. You will, of course, receive progress reports on the work done here. We will see to that."

Now he did jump from the chair. The sword clattered to the bare floor. Dukane looked down at it. Slowly, he brought his dark gaze back to Iroshi.

"You're just jealous of what I've managed to accomplish," he said in a low voice. "No one else got so far, not even you."

"Is that Dukane or his companion?" Iroshi asked Ensi silently.

*I cannot tell for sure,* Ensi answered. *They are so closely joined, and their shield does not weaken.*

"You're working yourself into trouble," she said aloud. "You may retire. Companions will be in touch through Paige."

"I don't want . . ." Dukane began.

"No more. We'll talk again before I leave."

He glared at her. She looked to the two guards standing at a distance, out of earshot but near enough to watch the scene closely. They had been warned there might be trouble, but even she had not expected any. Dukane's attitude was not surprising; however, his protests were as passionate as his love for the work he had been doing.

His gaze lowered at last, and he turned, picked up the sword, and stalked out of the guest quarters. The door banged shut behind him. The guards assumed a more relaxed posture, reminding her that she was also tensed for action. She took three deep breaths, felt her shoulders relax, and sat back in the chair.

So, they had definitely left him on this project much too long. It had been easy to do, since the work had progressed

# PERSEA

faster once he took over. If it were not for the other aspects of his tenure, she might have left him here forever. In spite of what she had told him, a few members did occupy positions for very long terms, but not often done.

Monitoring would have to be improved in the future to ensure nothing like this happened again. By the same token, Dukane would bear close watching from now on. The Iroshi cult he had spawned and his devotion to ferreting out Rune-Nelson's secrets might be fertile ground for mutiny within the ranks. It would be best to remove him from the planet as soon as possible.

*A Glaive racer is within two days' journey,* Ensi said. *Where should we send him?*

"I think back to Rune-Nevas for a rest and meditation. Perhaps a little reindoctrination would be in order, too."

*I will see to the arrangements.*

"Thanks."

Ensi would take care of those arrangements through his mind-link with other companions. The civilian employees of the Glaive knew to take their direction from many of the Glaive members, although not all had such authority The hierarchy had become as complicated in some instances as were the ceremonies, all of which she had either instigated or allowed.

She sighed. Somehow, things had not turned out exactly how she had envisioned them sixty years earlier. Along the way, she had lost control. But then, why should she be any different from other leaders?

Iroshi shook her head, wishing that the same thoughts and regrets would not keep returning. Whatever the Glaive had become was to her blame or credit. Even members like Dukane.

Time to forget all of that and concentrate on the problems on Djed. She would prefer to continue studying the reports on the work here, in spite of her impatience with some of the dry statistics and descriptions. However, the contract on Djed apparently required almost immediate attention.

"Ensi, is the racer being prepared for tomorrow morning?"

*Yes. By leaving tomorrow, we should arrive on Djed in thirteen days.*

"Is that soon enough?"

*It will have to be. I think Erik can keep events below the boiling point until then.*

"I'm sure he can."

She thought for a moment, wondering how such an apparently simple contract had become so complicated.

"This was a pro bono contract, wasn't it?"

*Yes. The scientists on Djed asked us to oversee the negotiations because they felt the Athenians were not dealing in good faith. A lot of third worlds fear being taken advantage of.*

"With good reason. Remember how the Altusians took advantage of the Verites."

*It was the Verites' fault, after all. They never once asked for Glaive assistance.*

"They didn't think they could afford our help. Not every world knows that we don't always work for the wealthiest."

*At least the Djedians thought to ask.*

"Anything further on this research project?"

*Essentially, all we know is that something other than the original goal has been achieved. The Djedians are staunch in their refusal to negotiate any further, and the Athenians still threaten war, claiming the Djedians never negotiated in good faith.*

That much they had learned from Erik. Plus the fact that both sides were demanding that Iroshi get involved herself.

"Without more information, I can't even begin to form a plan of . . ."

A loud bang on the door to the apartment cut off further discussion. One of the guards prepared to open it while the other prepared to defend. Iroshi's hand sought the hilt of her katana where it lay across the desk. The sword, which she had carried for decades, was rarely far from her hand.

When the door opened, Scanlon rushed in without even a glance at her protectors.

"Dukane's gone crazy," he said, more calmly than he appeared. "After he left you, he started toward his own quarters. The escort followed discreetly as you ordered. He suddenly bolted toward the east gate . . ."

"Ensi," Iroshi called silently.

"It's no use," Scanlon said. "His barrier is up. We can't get through."

*It is true,* Ensi confirmed. *He and Paige will not let anyone in.*

"Damn!" Iroshi said aloud. "How could we have misjudged him so badly? Both of them."

*We are not infallible . . .*

"Spare me the platitudes," she said silently, then aloud, "How many Glaive members can we completely trust here?"

Ensi and Scanlon's companion, Fotey, communed silently for a moment.

*At least half; around twenty.*

"Make sure the gates are sealed," she ordered. "Set up a search, using only those people we know we can trust. He knows this city and this world better than anyone else. If he gets free, we may never find him."

*There is also the problem of the booreecki,* Ensi said.

"What about them?"

*He knows them more than anyone else, too.*

Scanlon looked at her, then quickly away. Everyone in the Glaive knew of the first experience with the carnivores from this world, how their telepathic abilities had nearly paralyzed Iroshi and Erik Greer after they were marooned here. That and an attack by a creature known only as a mind vampire were the only two instances of such assaults within the Glaive. However they were enough to give any of them nightmares.

All right. Don't dwell on them. Action was needed, some of which was already set in motion by the silent orders from Ensi and Fotey. Iroshi was tempted to join in the search; she had once known the city fairly well herself, but that was before all the new construction. Scanlon had supervised some of the construction early in his career; another reason she had brought him along. After only a moment's hesitation, she instructed him to supervise the search personally.

"Keep me informed of your progress or lack of progress every moment," she ordered further. "He must be found. If he should break ranks . . ."

"True," Scanlon said, acknowledging the unspoken fear.

In the past, only death had taken members from the Glaive. A deserter could carry information to nonmembers that would jeopardize them all. Thank goodness this had not happened on a different world. At least all possible exits from Rune-Nelson were controlled by Glaive members.

"Lock down all ships for the moment, and check every port building. Dukane must not leave this world."

Scanlon nodded, waited another moment in case she thought of something else; then with another nod, he turned to go.

"Scanlon," she called. He stopped and looked back. "Did Dukane still have his sword?"

"Yes, he did."

She nodded. Before leaving, he stopped near the door, whispered to the guards a moment, then disappeared. His concern for her safety was relayed by Ensi. In her younger days, that might have meant he was in love with her; these days he might love her, but as one loves a mother or a mentor. The one thing Scanlon was not was overly ambitious. She had nothing to fear from him.

She forced herself to return to studying the records. Every so often, Ensi interrupted to report that there was nothing to report. At midnight, the same lack of progress was reported and she decided to head for bed. In spite of their insistence, Iroshi convinced the guards that they need not stay in her bedroom. Their own companions could monitor her and Ensi, probably detecting any intruder before he actually made it inside, even with a barrier up.

Maybe.

Protecting one's privacy had become more intricate and more reliable since the first companion and host melded. It had become more necessary as the membership grew and more people had the increased ability from two sensitive minds.

At that moment, her mind was turning to mush from fatigue. She finished undressing and climbed into bed.

"Lights out," she said, and the computer obeyed. Yes, things had changed radically. Particularly here on Rune-Nelson where she had once fought a huge snake-like creature on this floor of this very building.

She tried to relax, but thoughts kept actively rising and falling. Various possibilities came and went to explain Dukane's successfully avoiding detection. Even more possibilities about what his breakdown might mean to the Glaive.

Breakdown? Yes, that was the best description of what had happened. Hadn't he tested with the highest IQ of any initiate? In every bit of the training, he had been one of the quickest students. In spite of his size, he had been, and still was, graceful and fast. Very few had ever beaten him in training in the martial arts. Especially with a sword.

That was when she should have known that something might be wrong—when he chose his sword. She had forgotten—or at least, had not considered—the choosing for quite some time. Dukane had chosen the longest sword in the Glaive's collection. It had been one of the few times she had suspected a student's choosing had not occurred naturally. One of perhaps eight times.

The sword had once belonged to Johann August Heinrich Heros von Borcke, who, if she remembered correctly, lived in the nineteenth century. He had been quite a military man, largely ignored by historians, but well thought of by his peers. Standing six feet four inches tall, he was a giant of a man for his time, and the sword he had made of Damascus steel was a giant in its own right. Called the Great Pallasch, it was longer than any other in the vast collection.

In her relentless search for hand weapons, she had not only acquired this sword, she had also found an ancient text, a memoir written by the man himself. Although she did not remember all the details, they were always at hand if she needed them. As she had when Dukane chose the sword.

They stand before the door of the armory, just the two of them. Dukane towers over her. He is excited about the choosing of his sword, and he fidgets from one foot to the other. It makes him appear unusually clumsy.

"Relax," Iroshi says. "Listen as you enter the room. You will know which sword is the right one."

"How?"

He rubs his hands together. His self-confidence seems to be gone. In training, he has been best at the warrior skills. The mystic parts were difficult for him, as if he had no patience for them. The physical training, particularly sparring with a sword, has been the area in which he excelled. He will never be a truthsayer, but not all members can be.

"You will know," she says. "I can tell you no more than

that. Calm yourself. Take deep breaths. You should be receptive when you enter."

He does as she said, shaking his arms at his sides. Three deep breaths. He looks at her and smiles. She feels a touch of unease, but shrugs it away mentally. He has passed all the tests, met all the requirements, and his enthusiasm for membership is as great, maybe even greater, than that of most candidates.

She presses a button on the control box in her pocket, and the doors open. As far as the eye can see, row after row of racks stand. To the right, the racks bear swords of all descriptions and sizes. Every one is an antique or of special manufacture by modern craftsmen. To the left are other weapons: halberds, spears, knives; weapons sometimes used by Glaive members but mostly collected for their rarity and workmanship.

Dukane enters the room, looks to the left momentarily, then turns his attention to the swords. Unlike everyone else who has entered the room to select a sword, he does not look back at her when the voices make themselves heard. Does he not hear them, or is he just not surprised?

He looks over the racks directly in front of him, moving toward the back of the room. He moves to the next row and soon out of her sight. For a moment, Iroshi has the impression that he knows what he is looking for. A catalogue of the collection is available, but new members are not supposed to have access to it. The choosing is supposed to be a response to the voices, not a conscious choice.

Dukane is gone several moments. The slight sound of metal scraping against metal comes from the room and, in a few minutes, he reappears. He holds a sword and scabbard, and in an instant, she recognizes it. The Great Pallasch, difficult not to know because of its large size—the largest such weapon in the whole collection. It is reputed to be the largest ever made.

A smile lights his face. Clearly, he is pleased with his choice. Ensi can detect no reason to negate the choosing. It is done, then.

Reading over the account in her journal, Iroshi grew more and more convinced that the choosing had been a conscious one. However, since Ensi was unable to detect anything covert about the event at the time, it had stood.

She raised up on her elbows. Someone was near. Both a physical and a mental—no, an emotional—presence brushed her mind. Her hand once more sought the katana, this time on the table beside the bed.

*I feel it, too,* Ensi said. *However, it's very strange. It seems to be coming from the east wall.*

"Of course!" she said. "Think about the location of this room. Third floor. Near the old elevator shaft."

*The maintenance access doors.*

"It must be to the left of the bedroom door, on the east wall just as you're sensing." Iroshi listened a moment. "I assume he is still inaccessible."

*Yes.*

"Any tricks up your sleeve?"

*I will call the guards.*

"You should have done that already."

Ensi did not answer. He rarely appreciated being told of his failures or shortcomings. Of course, he had not called them until he was sure about what he sensed and where it came from. Rather, where *he* came from. Dukane had probably never gone far from the university building, hiding all this time in the same place she had used. More or less.

Iroshi swept the covers aside and, still gripping the handle of the sword, swung her feet to the floor. A panel slid back in the wall with a slight whoosh. Dukane moved into the room on near silent feet. Something clicked.

*He has locked the door.*

"Will he let the barrier down to fight?"

*I do not know.*

"Lights on," she said aloud.

The room was bathed in soft light. While both she and Dukane were partly blinded, she felt her way to the wall. His head moved in turn, keeping up, his eyes still blinking furiously. She could see now, so Ensi must be messing with the intruder's vision in spite of the barrier.

"Dukane," she said. She moved a few steps away from him. "You can't win. You're alone . . ."

"Alone, yes," he said as he tried to keep facing her as she moved again. "You've abandoned us, Iroshi. We would have followed you anywhere."

*Ah!* Ensi gasped. *He is pushing me out.*

"How?" she asked.

*He and Paige are stronger than we knew.*

Dukane and Iroshi stood still while their companions struggled. This was the first time such a struggle had ever happened within the ranks of the Glaive. The two guards beat on the door, hollered, called for help from others in the building. All the rebuilding had been done so well. And to Dukane's specifications.

A shout rose in her throat, a kiai, prelude to battle. Iroshi rushed forward, raising the sword, striking downward, meeting Dukane's blade. The ring of metal striking metal, the vibrations rushing from sword to arm to body . . .

Ensi and Paige lessened their grip on each other. Her strength, without Dukane's support, was not equal to Ensi's.

For Iroshi, the blow brought pain and exhilaration. Many years had passed since her last battle. Years of practice with passion, but no life and death in the balance. Dukane would not honor her aging body, humor her slowness in reacting, nor spare her life.

Their swords struck again. A red haze bathed the scene, and movement slowed. She might be older and slower, but she was experienced and still had a few tricks up her sleeve. They exchanged blows, and the red haze deepened. Dukane was just entering that phase as she started to enter the void. His confusion made her want to laugh. Paige tried to rally her host, and Iroshi wondered at the loss of cooperation between them. Sympathy rose in her breast until she became one with them. One with the swords. One with Ensi. One with the room, the building, the very air. The void: one thing Dukane had experienced but not mastered. One thing he had not sought with every waking moment, as she had when she was young and adventurous.

He backed away, stung by each blow from the katana. Sidestepping, he just avoided being backed up against the wall. Along the north wall, now, Iroshi rained blow after blow on his defense. Still backing away. Even in the void, she did not seek a killing blow. He was of the Glaive, a kinsman, and must be saved from his own foolishness.

Nearing the west wall in his retreat, Dukane stumbled against a chair. At the same moment, the bedroom door burst open and two guards fell into the room. Three more followed. Regaining their balance, the first two helped to form a semicircle behind Iroshi with the others.

"It's over," Iroshi said, bringing her sword to a rest position.

*We will not harm you,* Ensi added.

Dukane's expression grew calmer, the eyes half-veiled.

"Yes, it's over," he said.

With a cry he dashed for the window on his right and leapt through. Shattered mirglass surrounded him as his body began to fall.

*He has a plan . . .* Ensi began.

"I know," Iroshi said.

# 3

A ship on night watch is very quiet. Too quiet for those who cannot find sleep. And the older one gets, the more elusive sleep becomes. So Iroshi had discovered.

She had just left the bridge, intending to head for her cabin, but at the moment there was nothing to do there either. Everything had been finished earlier: reports checked and filed, orders given, and practice with the sword completed. In the relatively small cabin, she always used the shorter wakizashi; not as satisfying as the katana but sufficient.

At the end of the hall, she turned right instead of going into her cabin. Once more around. It would be wonderful if all this walking was enough to tire her out. One circuit would not have been enough on one of the old racers. They had been so small that walking the full circumference of the halls took about fifteen minutes. Now, this new racer—too big to be called that anymore—could take nearly half an hour. Twice as big as the old racer, but gods, was it faster!

She had always loved fast ships. Not that you could detect speed in space, but you could detect the passage of time, whether with a watch or clock or a schedule or your internal clock. Getting where she was going was always best when the trip could be made as fast as possible.

She passed Barnes, making his way toward the bridge. He saluted, and she guessed that the pilot must have the watch. Maybe he could not sleep either. Not likely, though. He was certainly young enough to sleep well.

Strange things to be thinking about. What she should be concentrating on was Djed and its scientists, but that was a bit of a dead end, too. According to the last report from Erik and Garon, the scientists were refusing to discuss anything at all until she got there. A very odd bunch of people, whether because they were from Djed or because they were scientists . . . A moot point at best. They were as they were, and that was what she and the Glaive would have to deal with.

And the negotiators from Athens had to deal with them, too. So far, they had exhibited a great deal of patience. How long that would last was anyone's guess, although their chief negotiator was reported to be very experienced.

There ended that line of consideration. Without more information on the nature of the work, and this sudden, unexpected change, she could make no plan of action, no decisions, no nothing. Once more she had been sorely tempted to allow an in-depth scan, but rules were rules. That step was taken only when absolutely necessary.

Just like her thoughts, her feet had brought her right back where she had started. Half an hour had passed and this time she opened the cabin door and went in. She leaned against the closed door, surveying this bit of her domain. Certainly larger than any cabin on this or any other Glaive racer. Still, it felt like a prison cell after the first three days. This trip was into its tenth day. Three more to go.

She eased herself into the easy chair with a sigh. Next damn ship she got would be as big as a small moon with room to run. And an observation hall with a huge window where she could watch the stars. Dream on. Such a ship was beyond even the resources of the Glaive.

*Still no sign of Dukane,* Ensi interrupted. He had a knack of knowing when this line of thought had gone far enough.

"I didn't expect there would be. He knew what he was doing every moment."

*It is not a total surprise.*

"No. We knew he was gifted, and we understood the problems that might occur in a person with so much talent and intelligence. We had to let him play it out. I only hope we don't regret our decision."

*He certainly was ready for us.*

"Indeed. More than we were ready for him. If only we can be sure that nothing happens to him."

*We have to find him first.*

"Oh, he'll show up again. I don't think it will be very much longer, either." She chuckled. "That window trick was pretty good, wasn't it?"

*You keep coming back to that. There have been a lot of guesses about how he did it but no one has actually figured it out.*

"I would have thought you knew," she said. Before Ensi could respond, she went on. "He has perfected levitation. or, at least he's better at it than most."

*I think you give him too much credit. Besides, we would have seen him on the ground if he had just lowered himself.*

"What if he went up to the roof? Or, he could have gone into any window above or below us. Even on the same floor. I suspect he went up, knowing that everyone would look down."

*Why did you not guess this at the time? We could have . . .*

"Even if we had known which way he went, we could not have caught him. Getting to the roof or the ground would have taken us a fair amount of time. Getting someone else there . . . Well, the roof was less likely to have people within close proximity."

She got up and started undressing.

"How is Scanlon coping?"

*In some ways he has the most peaceful spirit in the entire Glaive. He is working steadily, unperturbed by lack of success.*

"Good."

*He is mystified by something, though. As are many of us. Why would Dukane try to kill you at the same time he worships you? It would make better sense to try to convince you or even to accept that you might not be as perfect as he thought.*

"Not really. In his eyes, certain flaws are not to be tolerated. It was preferable for me to die a sort of martyr's death than to ruin the image he had created. It wasn't only my perfection that was endangered. His own was too. Those who follow him might not accept that he knows what he's talking about if I'm not the person he thought I was. My removing him from the project convinced him that I was not that person."

*Or changing into a different person.*

"That too."

She finished undressing, stretched, and climbed into the bed. The last things she had said had seemed a bit rambling. Maybe she was tired at last.

Erik Greer paced the reception area, wishing everyone would hurry up. Patience had never been his main strength, time was short, and his own self-confidence had shrunk over the last four weeks. He had been in the Glaive a long time, but this was the first time his efforts had been rebuffed. This kind of negotiation was his specialty, honed by years of successes.

That was what he should concentrate on: the successes. The present situation was unique and the turn of events not his fault. Still, it was his nature to take personal responsibility.

*Iroshi is coming,* Garon said.

Erik smiled in spite of himself. Seeing her, talking with her was always a pleasure, even when her mood was like thunder. He could not help feeling that just might describe her mood when she entered the reception area.

*She is calm and eager,* Garon continued.

Erik straightened his tunic and the double doors opened. Iroshi strode in, taking in the surroundings. It was often her alertness that people noticed first, although she could take on a lackadaisical air when the situation warranted it. She had quit wearing a cape some time ago and just afterward had taken to wearing a long skirt instead of slacks. For her arrival she had decided they would not wear dress uniforms and, while he had opted for royal blue, she wore pearl grey, her favorite color, under the long heavy coat. The uniform was only slightly darker than her hair, which at first glance looked as if she had cut it. Then she turned her head, and he could see the long ponytail hanging down her back.

Her eyes finally rested on him, and she smiled and held out her hand. He gripped it warmly. So often they went months without seeing each other, as in this case, and when they did meet, the happiness was always mutual.

Yet this time something else lay behind the happiness in her eyes. Something serious, disturbing.

"It's good to see you, Erik," Iroshi said.

"And you," he responded.

As he mulled over what Iroshi might be thinking, he shook hands with Jarys and Barnes, who had escorted Iroshi from the racer.

The racer's officers said their goodbyes and left for their quarters next to the port complex. He took her coat and handed it to one of the attendants as his own two bodyguards took their places.

Was it the trouble back on Rune-Nelson that bothered her? he wondered. Or the trouble here on Djed? Or both?

"I'm so glad to be back on solid ground," she said as he turned to lead the way out of the reception area. "We have much to talk about."

"Would you like to postpone meeting Guien Nole and the others?"

"No, we had better get that out of the way. We don't want to offend anyone just yet."

He recognized the edge to her voice that meant she was in no mood to play games with the likes of Djed's prime minister. The Djedians and the Athenians had better watch out. As they entered the wide hall, an honor guard fell in behind.

The audience hall was a fair distance from the reception hall and, as they walked, Iroshi told Erik of recent events on Rune-Nevas. Some things he had heard through Garon, but a lot was new to him. He tried to concentrate on what she said, but Iroshi's mood permeated her bearing and every word. Both were constant reminders that something was wrong. There was no indication that she was displeased with him, but this was one of the few times she had been called in because negotiations were failing.

No matter what disturbed her, he would have to wait at least another hour to find out. They turned right, and at the end of the next hall, two gaily uniformed soldiers stood on either side of another pair of large double doors. These guards snapped to attention, and when the group drew near they pulled the doors open. Erik fell a pace behind as they entered the hall.

At the opposite end of the room a dazzling welcoming committee of nine people stood in a semicircle. Most of their suits and uniforms were in jewel colors—green, blue, gold. For a third world, Djed had well-dressed officials. This might be a third-class world, but they managed to put on a first-class show. They were certainly going all out for the head of the Glaive.

Iroshi stopped just in front of the man in the center of the waiting line.

"Iroshi, may I present Guien Nole, prime minister of Djed," Erik said.

The prime minister smiled and held out his hand. Iroshi shook it warmly, saying how much she had looked forward to meeting him. Nole introduced the rest of the Djedian officials and, last, he introduced Dr. Senta Drace, head of the research party, and one of only two women representing her planet.

"Is the Athenian representative not here?" Iroshi asked.

"I'm afraid not," Nole said. "We thought she would be, but . . ." He shrugged. "May we invite you to dine with us? Our late meal is simple, but we would be pleased if you would join us."

She nodded.

"I would be honored," she said. "However, if it won't offend anyone, I will make it a brief meal. I'm eager to get settled in."

"No offense will be taken," Nole said.

Everyone else mirrored his smile as he turned toward the small state dining room. Erik took his place behind Iroshi as they all began moving off, with the two Glaive bodyguards behind him.

The food was good and the company agreeable. Erik watched, fascinated as always, with the ways in which people endeavored to be pleasant in Iroshi's company. By now, almost everyone knew that the Glaive was a powerful organization and with whom to curry favor. He had seen the mention of her name bring a more amenable attitude to many intractable negotiators. That had not always been the case, but it was rare now that anyone took her presence lightly.

By asking questions, Iroshi kept conversation going for nearly half an hour, then she made her excuses. Erik retrieved their coats and escorted her to the underground garage, explaining on the way that it would be so much warmer than having the car wait outside the main entrance. Once there, the two bodyguards climbed into a car and left for the house assigned to the Glaive. Then he introduced her to Jacob, their driver, and Floyd, his personal bodyguard, both of whom were longtime civilian employees of the Glaive.

"Didn't you work with me on Alondro a few years ago?" she asked Jacob.

"Yes, I sure did," he said. "A short assignment, but interesting."

"Yes. The Alondrons weren't too happy about that air car we wrecked." Jacob grinned, and she turned to Floyd. "I don't think we've ever worked together directly before."

"No, ma'am. I've been working mostly with the warriors . . . uh, bodyguards on those assignments. This is my first contract assignment."

"Different, isn't it?"

"Yes, ma'am."

He cut his eyes toward Jacob, as if to assure himself that he was behaving all right. His cohort kept his eyes straight ahead, which must have been the signal that all was well, for he grinned slightly and looked back at Iroshi.

"Let's get to the house," Erik said.

Floyd held the back door for her and Erik. He and Jacob climbed into the front seat. Jacob started the car and guided it up the exit ramp and out into the black night. The use of ground cars rather than air cars had been one oddity about Djed that had interested her. She rarely got to ride in one and had forgotten the difference in the smoothness of the ride. Not that air cars always rode more smoothly; just that the bumps were less solid.

The ride to the house did not take long. Called Godolphin House, it was one of several along Chance Street that were reserved for visiting dignitaries of whatever rank who chose to visit such an out-of-the-way world.

"It's quite warm, and we've installed our own security," Erik explained as the car halted in front of a two-story building resembling a Victorian clapboard house on Earth. "Their technology isn't the best, overall."

"They do take their history seriously here, don't they?" she commented.

"Yes, they do. From their religion to their fashions. Most of them have some connection with ancient Egypt, though."

"Victorian?"

"The Victorians were big into artifacts and all that. They used a lot of Egyptian motifs." Iroshi smiled at him. "They love to tell everyone about it," he said with a grin. "I've learned more Earth history here than I did in school."

"Good for you," she said, and they climbed out.

Jacob and Floyd followed as they walked up the sidewalk to the door of the house. Her breath showed in the night air, backlit by light from the windows. She shivered slightly. It had been a long time since she had experienced a real winter. The temple on Rune-Nevas was located on the edge of a desert, and most of the rest of her home world was hot and arid. Only the polar regions experienced true winter, although it was mostly cold wind. Snow rarely fell, something Erik had said they could expect almost any time on Djed, now that their autumn had arrived.

"Your suite and my bedroom are upstairs," he said as they passed between the two guards and went inside.

They said goodnight to Jacob and Floyd, who would take turns keeping watch inside during the night, along with the guards, and Erik led the way upstairs. The suite consisted of a sitting room and a bedroom with another connecting bedroom. Erik explained that his room was on the other side of the hall, Jacob's was next to his, and Floyd's next to that. The support staff had rooms on the first floor.

Harleq, her steward, stood in the sitting room. He had taken care of her clothes and other luggage and waited until she arrived to make sure she needed nothing else. Once assured that everything was fine, he disappeared downstairs. She sat on the sofa, still prone to folding her feet under her. Since the day was nearly over, Erik offered her some wine from the cooler. She accepted a glass of local red vintage that was one of his personal favorites. They sat together in silence for several minutes, sipping the wine. He felt her relax, and was able to relax himself as warmth spread from his stomach to the rest of his body.

"No one brought up the business at hand during dinner," she said suddenly.

"It isn't considered proper to discuss business at table," he explained.

She nodded and took another sip. The silence lengthened. Clearly, she was listening to Ensi for part of that time.

"Well," she said. "You and I need to discuss everything that's been happening here. But first, let's talk about Dukane and what happened on Rune-Nelson."

Iroshi turned off the shower, and the drying lamp came on. Within two minutes, both her body and her hair were dry. She gathered her hair under a cap, and a moisturizing spray covered every inch of her skin. She stepped out, removed the cap, and pulled on her robe.

Most of the tension in her shoulders and neck was gone. The bed was going to feel especially good. It had been a long night. After hearing about Dukane and his escape, Erik had insisted on discussing security measures being taken. Like everyone else in the Glaive, he felt that Dukane was a definite threat to her. His concern was touching and very appreciated.

After two, she had sent him to his own suite, too tired to talk about another change in security or anything else. He went through the door, and within two heartbeats she had gotten into the shower. And now, she would crawl into that bed and . . .

Outside, a woman screamed.

Vague sounds of a struggle came through the main door of the suite when Iroshi emerged from the bedroom, sword in hand.

*. . . there is nothing to sense,* Ensi was saying.

She rushed downstairs, where everyone was beginning to gather in front of the main door. Someone yelped outside. Harleq got between Iroshi and the door, his pistol pointed up, looking ready to do battle with her or for her, whichever he deemed necessary in order to protect her. She stopped. Anger rose, and she gripped the sword tighter.

*Let it go,* Ensi said soothingly. *He is not the one with whom to do battle.*

As she stood still, Harleq edged toward the door. He activated the screen and looked at the image a moment, hand poised above the touch pad.

*The guards have her. She is hard to control, but she poses no real threat.*

Harleq touched the pad, and the door swung open. A woman struggled in the arms of both guards. She screamed again, a sound made more horrible by the total lack of expression on her face.

# 4

Everyone stood in the entry hall. The prisoner, arms held by the guards, was quiet now, the same dull expression on her face. It had been a real struggle to get her inside; she was stronger than her frail figure would indicate. She wore no coat or hat, only a dress of some lightweight material.

"Do you know her?" Iroshi asked Erik.

She touched the woman's arm. The skin was unbelievably cold.

"She looks a little like a woman I met," he answered. "But it isn't her."

*There is nothing in her mind,* Ensi said, confirming his earlier impression.

"Nothing at all?" she asked.

*No thoughts. No personality. She is an empty shell.*

"Why did she fight the guards so hard?"

*Basic instinct, I would guess.*

"It's almost impossible to believe," she said aloud. "Not even madness leaves a person so empty."

She glanced at the guards, assuring herself that she had spoken too softly for them to overhear. Looking back, she caught Erik watching the prisoner intently.

"The woman she resembles . . . how closely, would you say?"

"Very closely. It's uncanny. Maybe it's the lifelessness that makes the difference."

"We aren't going to find out anything from her," she

said. "Get in touch with some official who can take care of her."

They all moved into the great room and Erik made a call on the comm system set into the bar. He joined Iroshi on the sofa while the guards remained near the door, still holding onto their charge. Floyd and Jacob had gone outside to check the grounds. Harleq stood near the sofa, listening for the door signal, and watching everyone in the room.

The young woman stood quietly the entire time, her face blank, her posture slumped. All of the fight appeared to have gone out of her. Iroshi studied her, wanting to understand what the hell was going on. She looked to be about thirty-five. Her black hair was cut short and close to the scalp all around. Her skin was pale and clear, like a newborn baby's, and almost translucent. If you looked hard enough, you might see the blood coursing through her veins.

Her face was lovely, the features finely sculpted, the eyes... The eyes were very large, dark brown, almost as dark as her hair. So large and so dead. Not one spark of life shone from them.

*Someone is coming,* Ensi said.

"Who?"

*You will be surprised.*

"You're supposed to make sure I'm not surprised," she said impatiently.

Before she could demand the name, the door chimed. Harleq moved back to the entry hall and pushed the button on the door control panel. He studied the image on the small screen, then looked at Iroshi. His left eyebrow arched. He touched the pad, and the door slid open to admit Senta Drace instead of someone from security as they had all expected. The scientist rushed into the room, heading straight toward the sofa, Floyd and Jacob close behind.

Iroshi and Erik got to their feet, Erik placing himself a little in front of her. Harleq followed closely behind.

"I came as soon as I could," Drace said breathlessly, apparently unaware of their defensive postures. "Iroshi, I am so sorry this happened. She wanders off occasionally but has never gone this far before."

"Is she your patient?" Iroshi asked.

"Yes," Drace answered. "Well, I do some work at the sanitarium. I am a medical doctor and a psychiatrist."

"What is her name?"

"Uh, Prilly Jaxe."

"She hasn't said a word," Iroshi said. "What is her diagnosis?"

"Catatonic schizophrenia. She hasn't spoken a word for almost twenty years. Not since she was a child, I'm afraid."

"How sad. She is very pretty. And strong. She gave my men quite a struggle."

"It's an aversion to being held. She has always been that way." Drace rubbed her hands together. "But it's late and I should get her back."

*All lies,* Ensi said. *Do you want me to probe?*

"Just surface examination, please," Iroshi said silently. "We don't want to give ourselves away just yet."

*Of course.*

"Can we offer any assistance" she said aloud. "One of the guards?"

"No, thank you. Prilly is not difficult, and my driver is waiting outside. We will be quite safe."

She moved to the girl, took hold of her arm, and started leading her toward the door.

"I appreciate your help," Drace said, then left the house.

Iroshi stood watching the two moving down the sidewalk toward a waiting car.

"I'm beginning to think these people are involved in something much too dangerous," Iroshi said.

She nodded to Harleq, who relaxed slightly, sent the guards back onto the porch, and closed the door. After making sure it was locked and visually checking the room one more time, he nodded to Iroshi and disappeared toward his own room. She climbed the stairs and dropped onto the sofa in the sitting room with a sigh that came from the pit of her stomach. Her eyes burned, and she rubbed them with the heels of her hands. Gods, she was tired. Too tired to sleep for a while. Erik looked as wired as she felt.

"How about some wine?" she said. "Or tea, maybe."

"Something hot would taste better right now," he said. He started toward the bar.

"I'll get it," she said. "I need to move a little bit more."

She got up, moved to the replicator, and stood looking at it. After a moment, the combination came to her for Darjeeling tea and she input the code—hot and with sugar. The two mugs filled from the spigot, and she carried them to the sofa.

They drank half of the hot liquid before either of them spoke. Ensi and Garon remained quiet. She consciously cleared her mind and took control of the random thoughts, tucking them down to leave space for the current issue.

"All right, Ensi," she said aloud so that Erik heard. "What did you get from Doctor Drace?"

*She was lying, of course,* he said. *But only about Prilly Jaxe and her illness. The woman was totally perplexed about how the woman got here. She does wander off from time to time, but has never gone far from the sanitarium.*

"Was there anything from Prilly when Drace arrived?"

*No reaction whatever. There is neither mind nor soul in that body.*

"A clone?" Erik said.

"I wouldn't think so," Iroshi said. "A clone is supposed to be a duplicate of the person the DNA was taken from."

"But the mind is still in the original body. The reason I

think it might be possible is the person this Prilly resembles. It came to me when Drace was leading her away. She is a younger version of Lisley Nole, the prime minister's wife."

"Her sister, maybe?"

"No, she has two brothers, both members of the advisory council, but no other family."

"She has no children?"

"There has been talk of a child somewhere, but no one really knows."

"Prilly might be her daughter, then. That would explain the resemblance, but not the confinement in an institution."

*That should not be difficult to check out,* Ensi said. *Garon and I can do that tonight while everyone sleeps.*

"Which I think I'm ready for," Iroshi said.

She stretched and yawned, and Erik stifled a yawn of his own.

"Since there are no meetings until tomorrow afternoon, I'm going to sleep in," she said. "Come by around noon, Erik, and you can brief me."

"Yes, Iroshi," he said. He kissed her cheek and stood up. "I'll see you tomorrow."

"Goodnight."

She watched him until the door shut. It was difficult sometimes to realize that he was in his sixties, now. He still kept that body in good shape, just like his brother, Mark, who taught in Crowell's dojo in Japan back on Earth. She had no doubt that they kept in touch daily; in the early days of their service, they had been inseparable. She wondered how their wives handled that. Quite often there was jealousy under those circumstances.

None of her business, really. Glaive members' private lives were their own business. However, it was important for the well-being of the Glaive as a whole that there be as little dissension as possible. Erik and Mark should have less trouble than most: Erik's wife, Sheera, was a member of the Glaive, and Lori, Mark's wife, was with him on Earth.

Her thoughts turned from the Greer brothers back to the recent, puzzling event.

"Did Drace and her charge make it back safely?" she asked Ensi.

*Yes, they just arrived.*

"Good. I'm off to bed, then."

The next morning she awoke at nine, irritable at not being able to sleep later. Four or five hours' sleep just was not enough. She tried not to snap at Harleq and succeeded most of the time. He had grown accustomed to her moods over the years, but she did not like that side of herself. Like most people, she was prone to take her temper out on those closest to her. Somehow, Iroshi should be above that sort of pettiness.

*Now you are doing it,* Ensi said.

"Doing what?"

*Setting yourself above other people. Treating yourself...*

"All right," she snapped.

*You have always expected more of yourself than you do of other people. You are only human, you know.*

"Yes, I know."

*I would say that others come by Iroshi-worship honestly.*

She laughed out loud.

The night air was cool and humid, evidenced by his breath rising into the shaft of light thrown ahead by his torch. At least the autumn winds were not yet blowing. Dukane hurried toward the clearing and shelter. He was in a good mood. This was the final night for preparation. In two days' time he would leave Rune-Nelson, his home for fifteen years, and might never return. He would leave behind his following and his beloved booreecki, all but two of them that is. Sandoval and Vieren would go with him. After all, he had raised them from pups and had no intention of giving them up.

Dammit, none of this would have been necessary if Iroshi had continued playing her part. She was born to greatness, to be revered, and she squandered her gifts. It was his task to put everything right. He accepted that readily, for his was the vision that would guide her, remind her of her responsibilities to him and the others.

The clearing came into view just ahead. He stopped, reached out with his mind for any threatening presence near the ship. All clear, but in that instant, he felt the slight touch of a companion, searching, trying to detect his thought patterns. Only a momentary touch. Paige, always on guard, closed the barrier around her hosts' probe, concentrating it, ensuring that there was little danger of detection.

Dukane moved into the clearing, but stopped short. Ahead, two pairs of red spots gleamed in the light of the torch. They flickered, then remained steady, directed at him. No other details were revealed by the light until, with a growl, two dark forms detached themselves from the shadows around the racer.

"No, you don't!" Dukane cried.

He broke into a run toward the ship, at an angle to the approaching shapes. He thumbed a pad on the wrist control and the door slid up, disappearing into the hull. Just a little faster and he would reach it. With another growl, one of the four-legged beasts leapt, catching him in the middle of the back. Dukane fell face forward, the wind knocked out of him for a moment. The second beast ran up and began licking his face while the first at last stepped off his back.

Catching his breath, Dukane laughed, reaching toward the female and pulling her close. She continued licking his face, washing him free of dirt that clung there. The male stood back, watching the two, trying to turn the man's attention from his mate.

"All right, Sandoval, no need to be jealous," Dukane said, knowing that was not at all true.

One day the male booreecky would not get off his back. Vieren would do everything she could to protect the man, even from her own mate, but Sandoval was bigger and stronger than she. They would find out which would win when the inevitable confrontation between the two males in her life came about.

Vieren finished cleaning his face and sat on her haunches.

"Time to be fed, I suppose," Dukane said as he sat up. "You two have gotten lazy. Why aren't you out there hunting for your food?"

It was an idle accusation, since they hunted only when he allowed them. That he did infrequently.

He got to his feet and led them into the ship. Both of the booreecki danced and skipped behind, one happy to have the man back, both happy at the prospect of being fed. Since taking them from their mother, right after birth, Dukane had been the only parent they had known. He had worked with them, trained them for his own needs. The most important part of that training had been aimed at their telepathic abilities. They used them only when he approved—no, when he ordered them to do so. Their telepathy was strongly linked to their hunting.

Once in the galley, Dukane pulled out a pouch of ground meat and dumped the contents into two large bowls, which he put on the floor. He watched as they devoured the meals. The fawn-colored male and his harlequin-coated mate ate it all in a few minutes; the special blend of flavors was the only solid food they had ever eaten. Their pleasure seeped into his mind. Their tufted ears stood upright on the tops of their heads, a sign of their satiation and contentment.

Finished, Vieren sat in front of him and raised her right

front paw. Dukane took it in his right hand. Her prehensile thumb wrapped around the back of his hand as he had taught them to do when "shaking hands." Sandoval sat near the water dish, watching, a large dose of jealousy escaping through his thought barrier.

As with people, not all booreecki were telepathic, although the percentage compared to the total population was higher among the carnivores. From the beginning, they had proved easily trainable in every aspect, including suppressing the transmission of thought. Most did not receive thoughts from humans easily. Sandoval and Vieren were two exceptions, and their talents had been enhanced through hours of training. And it was now time to practice.

Both animals stood up. They sensed he was ready before Dukane moved. Just as they always did. It was a favorite time of the day for all of them. This time, they would continue with the new parameters. He led the way to his own cabin, where more room and privacy could be guaranteed, although the need might be less on the racer than it had been back in the university. Only two others knew of this ship's existence and its current location, and neither of them was due tonight. Still, caution was most effective when practiced often.

Not much longer before he and his compatriots would be able to leave Rune-Nelson. The time was close for salvaging their cause. Everything must be ready.

# 5

✧

Lenora Cieras sat on one side of the circular table, flanked by two aides: Logan Rhiel and Anton Merriel. The head of the Athenian delegation was the nervous sort, constantly picking at her sleeves, squirming in her chair, blinking her eyes rapidly. Her blonde hair was cut short, probably to keep her from twirling strands around her fingers, Iroshi thought. Still, her short, thin fingers kept pulling at a strand that fell onto her forehead.

Her whole being was thin, even her voice that could probably take on a whining tone very easily. Even so, there was a quality about her that kept the voice from becoming an irritant, something in her personality and her sense of style. The expensive suit of rare Ganian silk was plainly made. Her eyes were bright, constantly moving, and amazingly blue. Probably color-enhanced.

Earlier at brunch, Erik had given his impression of Cieras.

"At first, she seems ill-suited to negotiating because of her nervous nature," he had said. "But, it turns out that she's tough and single-minded. The problem is, she's accustomed to negotiating from a position of strength. In this case, it's the Djedians who seem to have the stronger position. Right now, she's frustrated as hell. The Djedians have stopped talking. Cieras has tried to be patient, but I understand that she's asked her government to recall her and send someone else."

"What about the people who work for her?" Iroshi asked.

"There's no personal loyalty, but they are loyal to Athens. As Cieras is."

"So none of them would have leaked word about the negotiations?" Erik shook his head. "Who called the Glaive in?" Iroshi continued.

"Djed. However, Athens agreed, once they knew others were interested in the discovery."

"How could anyone else be interested if no one knows what the hell it is?"

Erik shrugged.

The original discovery may have become known, and several powers would be interested in that, of course. However, if the Glaive did not know what the new turn was, no one else should have gotten details either. The negotiations had been difficult, bogging down at regular intervals. That was quite ordinary, especially when the two sides were unequal in strength. Sitting across from Cieras now, Ensi got much the same impression that Erik had relayed.

"Has she ever seen Prilly Jaxe?" Iroshi asked silently.

The question startled Ensi—it was totally unexpected—and he did not answer at once.

*I found no surface memory of the young woman.*

"Search a little deeper, please."

*All right.*

"You agreed to the Glaive's entering the negotiations," Iroshi said aloud.

"Yes, but we had no idea how much this would slow everything down," Cieras said. The Athenian had been voicing complaints over progress in general, and the length of time they had been waiting for Iroshi's arrival specifically.

"We have first rights to this formula," Cieras went on. "They offered us the opportunity to back the research and the marketing, and we accepted. All we want now is for the Djedians to negotiate with us in good faith."

"A formula to prolong life is a very important product," Iroshi said. "There are those who would like to keep it for themselves. Others would prefer to sell it to make huge fortunes, build empires. The Djedians—at least the government—want to use the formula, to raise themselves from third-world status. Are you certain that you and they are strong enough together to keep it for yourselves? Perhaps a third partner would make things easier. Or a fourth."

"A third partner? The Glaive, for instance?"

"No, we are restricted by contract and our own rules from becoming a partner in this venture. Our role is strictly that of mediator."

"But you could participate if you wanted to. After all, they are your rules."

Cieras pushed at the strand of hair on her forehead again. However, most other nervous habits had vanished. This was the kind of verbal sparring she thrived on.

"Only if both parties currently negotiating requested it and certain conditions were met," Iroshi said. "We don't use our presence to further aggrandize our guild."

"So, your purpose here is . . ."

"To assist in reaching an amicable agreement that will work for many years. The very reason we were called in."

"Yes, of course."

Cieras's immediate goal was to bring the talks back on track, to get what she came for. She would probably offer the Glaive a percentage, perhaps even free access to the formula. The question was, which would serve the Glaive best: the profits, or not risking any smudge on the reputation of the guild she had spent so many years building? This was the reason her presence had been requested. They must have decided that Erik could not make any commitment for the Glaive and that he would not accept a bribe for himself. Like most people in positions of authority, they figured everyone had her price.

Cieras placed the palms of her hands flat on the tabletop and leaned forward.

"Iroshi, let me speak plainly," she said. "My world wants this contract. For reasons I can't go into—"

*They are about to lose the Aldebaran mining rights,* Ensi interjected.

"—it is important for us to get this contract. I can say that we are looking for ways to expand into other areas. As you know, we are strong in mining and manufacturing."

*If they lose those mining rights, the factories on Athens will have to go elsewhere for the raw minerals. A more costly source, of course.*

"Unfortunately, when the talks came to a sudden halt, neither your Mr. Greer nor I could budge Drace or Nole. Nor could we get an explanation of why. We did find out that the experiments had taken an unexpected turn, as I'm sure Mr. Greer told you."

Iroshi nodded.

"Now that you are here, is there any way you can see to get things moving again? At the rate we are going right now, this could take a year or more instead of months."

"That is why I'm here," Iroshi said.

"Is there anything I can do to speed things along?"

"Only have patience."

"Oh, I was thinking perhaps I might suggest offering you—or the Glaive—a partnership."

Iroshi stood. Cieras had finally come right out and said it.

"That would be inappropriate, Lenora Cieras, at this time," Iroshi said. The Athenian smiled and got to her feet too. "Now, if you'll excuse me," Iroshi continued, "I have other meetings to prepare for."

Cieras came around the table; her aides had also stood

when she did, and they now remained where they were. Jacob opened the door of the small conference room.

"Of course, Iroshi of the Glaive. I look forward to meeting with you again."

They shook hands, Cieras still smiling. Iroshi nodded and stepped into the hall where Erik and Floyd were waiting. The bodyguard dropped behind as they walked down the hallway.

"Ensi kept me up on the meeting," he said. "You know that by calling Cieras by her full name you have indicated your willingness to talk about a bribe, don't you?" he asked.

"Why, Erik! All I did was follow her lead and try to put our relationship on a less formal basis."

Erik grinned.

"Yes, but with the Athenians, timing is everything," he said.

"Is it, now? How interesting. Do you think I may have given Cieras the wrong impression?"

"Could be," he said, shaking his head. "If the Djedians find out, they will be very angry."

"I'm sure they will find out. One way or another."

*She knew nothing of Prilly Jaxe,* Ensi said just as she was going to ask. *Neither the name nor the young woman's appearance.*

"Why did we meet her?" she wondered aloud.

They walked in silence a moment. As they turned a corner, Iroshi touched Erik's arm.

"What did you learn at the sanitarium?"

"The people who work there are very close-mouthed," he said. "They wouldn't even tell me if Prilly got back safely last night."

He paused as they passed someone going the opposite direction. It suddenly struck Iroshi how deserted the hallway was.

"I did confirm she is there," he continued. "There is a special ward. Apparently she isn't the only patient with her particular affliction."

"How many?"

"Difficult to tell. At least three. There could be many more."

They had reached the suite that had been assigned them when they were between meetings in the palace. The main and larger meetings were held in a building called Rohbins Conference Hall nearly a mile away. Ensi probed the rooms, making sure no one waited inside.

"Could Garon find them?" Iroshi asked.

Ensi declared the room clear, and she opened the door.

"Nothing from any of them," Erik said.

Once inside, he adjusted his wrist unit to scan for listening devices or cameras. Because of scattered statuary and numerous other decorations, the central room afforded numerous hiding places. Furniture was sparse, though: a semicircular sofa in a cream-colored imitation leather plus three matching chairs arranged so that they, with the sofa, completed a lopsided circle; three tables provided space for anyone sitting in the room to set a drink. These pieces stood out strongly against the plush royal blue carpet. Floor-to-ceiling drapes partially covering the windows on the opposite wall matched the furniture in color. The only other color in the room was from the brass of the chandelier, the finials on the curtain rods, and the control panels for lights and communication. A definite attempt at elegance that did not quite make it. Like so much of Djed.

Erik gave a thumbs-up and moved into the second room. Iroshi settled on the sofa to wait.

*Company,* Ensi announced.

A moment later, the door chimed. Erik came from the other room to answer. Floyd announced: "His Holiness, Patriarch Roman."

"One moment," Erik said. He closed the door and looked to her.

"You seem surprised," she said.

"I am. He rarely leaves the temple. It seems that everyone wants to meet you."

She could hardly keep the head of the major Djedian religious organization waiting in the hall, but she always dreaded meeting such people. Religious leaders, or, indeed, anyone of a devout nature were always so narrow-minded, especially people from those orders based on ancient Earth religions. This one was taken from one of the oldest of all, and probably managed to misinterpret the original like so many others.

*I will protect you,* Ensi said with a chuckle.

"Of course you will," she said silently. Then, aloud to Erik, "Let him in, please."

Erik nodded and opened the door. The Patriarch was preceded by two men in deep blue, flowing robes. His holiness walked in, swathed in an equally blue robe plus a matching turban trimmed in silver. He moved in that obsequious yet pompous manner so typical of people of his ilk. He approached Iroshi and held out his hand.

"Iroshi, how wonderful to finally meet you," he said in a pleasant baritone that must be a great asset in his work. The hand hovered, and the dark side of her wanted to leave it dangling, untouched, unacknowledged.

*He expects you to kiss the ring,* Ensi announced.

"I know," she replied. "I suppose I will have to do something."

She took his hand in her own strong grip and shook it. He raised an eyebrow in surprise. The priests appeared to be scandalized. She released the hand.

"Won't you have a seat, Your Holiness?" she said.

He nodded, the gleaming turban reflecting light from the chandelier. She would bet almost anything that he was bald under it.

He took one of the chairs, the priests arranging themselves behind him. She resumed her seat on the sofa, Erik deciding at the last minute to stand behind her in imitation of the visitors.

"I am sorry that I was unable to attend the dinner when you arrived last night," Roman said. "I seldom leave the temple except on holy days."

"Then you honor me today."

He waved away the flattery.

"My motives are rather selfish. I have heard so much about the head of the Guild of the Glaive that I just had to see for myself."

"And are you disappointed?"

"No, not at all. Although I will grant you that everything I have heard has not been entirely complimentary."

"One does not gain such notoriety without having lived an active life. Would you care for something to drink?"

"Wine would be nice," he said.

"And your priests?"

He smiled slightly, as if it was a child's question.

"Nothing for them. They are on duty."

Erik got the drinks, wine for the Patriarch and tea for her. Roman took a sip.

"Ah, one of our own," he said.

"We appreciate Djedian wines," Iroshi said.

"No, I meant one of the wines we make and bottle at the temple. Our varieties are the most important exports from Djed. Unfortunately, it's one product we cannot sell more of because the farmers cannot expand their vineyards. Good soil is something of a rarity, you see."

"The growers must appreciate the income."

"The grapes are their contribution to the temple."

"Then the temple appreciates the income."

"It all goes to support our many charities and projects designed to benefit our people."

His smile broadened.

"I'm certain you and your followers do much good work," she said.

He nodded again. Then he pointed at her sword which lay across her knees.

"Do you have that with you at all times?"

"Yes. Although they are still quite functional, our swords are more part of the uniform these days."

"I see. Still, it seems belligerent."

She laughed. "Of course it does."

Roman frowned, displeased that his comment had been taken so lightly. She recalled that the temple had been instrumental in getting guns banned from Djed and, clearly, he had meant it as a criticism.

*The Patriarch also disapproves of the research on persea in the first place,* Ensi commented. *On religious grounds, of course.*

"Of course," Iroshi responded silently.

*However, if the research continues, and persea is marketed in some way, he believes that he and the temple should have some part in it.*

"The profits, you mean. Like the wine."

*Oh, yes. And a say in who gets to take the magic formula and live forever. To him and others like him, such powers belong to the followers of the gods.*

"By whatever name she is called."

"In any event," Roman was saying, "I felt that we should meet. Our government has not taken into account all of the ramifications of this research, and I hope to convince you that we should be consulted on several different aspects of these negotiations."

"On whose behalf do you speak?" Iroshi asked.

"The temple's, of course. Most of our people follow our teachings."

"Do you resent Djed's need for help from others?" she prodded further.

"Not at all. We all recognize that for the time being Djed is not one of the more powerful of the independent worlds. Like every other Djedian, we would like to see that condition changed and have high hopes that the discovery of this new formula will help achieve that end result."

Erik leaned down from behind and said softly, "The meeting with Guien Nole begins in fifteen minutes."

"I am sorry, Your Holiness, but I am reminded that I have a meeting to attend soon." She stood. "Perhaps we can meet again and discuss the appropriate role for the temple."

Roman's expression turned bland, but annoyance tightened his movements as he too stood up.

"We must," he said. "We insist on having a role. There are too many implications . . ."

"Yes, I know," she interrupted. She started toward the door. "I am sure that your government knows how important it is that your input be considered in these negotiations and the final agreement. We will do everything we can to ensure nothing important is left out."

Erik opened the door, and Floyd took his place beside the opening. Annoyance had turned to anger within the Patriarch's mind, and his heartbeat increased. Outwardly, though, he maintained his composure remarkably well.

"I apologize again, Your Holiness, for this abrupt end to our conversation. We must try to meet again soon."

This time she held out her hand first. He took it in his own and held it.

"Yes, we must," he said. With a swish of his robes he left the room, his escort hard put to keep up.

Erik closed the door once again.

"Volatile, isn't he?" Iroshi said.

"He is known to have a temper," Erik agreed.

"Their religion is a combination of Old Earth Christianity and ancient Egyptian, isn't it?"

"The rites and names of the gods are based on the more ancient religion. Their stated belief of helping others and living in peace is supposed to be Christian."

"Wasn't Christianity supposed to be monotheistic?"

"Essentially, yes."

"I wonder how they managed to reconcile the two?" She retrieved her sword and slung it across her back. "We had best get to this meeting. Now, I get to see the Djedians and Athenians together. It should prove interesting."

"Yes, it should," Erik said. "It certainly should."

# 6

❖

The laboratory was quiet. Most of the technicians had been sent home before the visitors arrived. Computers sat silent. Workstations, not quite clean, looked recently abandoned, the surroundings clear evidence that the visit had been hastily planned.

Iroshi felt oddly uncomfortable as she stood just inside the doorway. She half-expected something to move as if the people were still here, but going about their work invisibly. Acrid odors from their last experiments hung in the air, a feeling of pending results attached to them. She disliked laboratories like this. At least, she did now that she was older. When she was under forty, she had enjoyed what seemed the challenge of experimentation, the thrill of discovery, but one day, for whatever reason, there had seemed to be more menace than promise. Which was very silly, since both were aspects of people rather than of chemicals and potions.

Senta Drace, having led the way into the crowded room, waited at the far end for everyone to come through the door and find a place to stand. Those unaccustomed to being in such an atmosphere—which included most of them—crossed their arms or held their clothes tight against their bodies to keep from brushing fragile containers to the floor. Guien Nole seemed the most uncomfortable. Erik, staying close to Iroshi as usual, was the calmest. Lenora Cieras, most careful not to touch anything, had the air of one who had been in the room many times but trusted none of what it contained. Iroshi's two guards, the three aides accompanying Nole, and two more with Cieras made up the rest of the company of visitors.

At last, all seemed to have arrived and settled as best they could. Drace cleared her throat, and everyone quieted. She studied a handheld viewer for a moment, then raised her head, looking around the room at everyone.

"Thank all of you for agreeing to visit here again," she said. "We thought it would be good for Iroshi to see where most of the work has been done on persea, but we did not want to exclude everyone else."

They had all met in a large conference room in the palace first. There had been some talk, mostly about bringing Iroshi up to date on what had transpired thus far. Out of the blue, Drace had suggested that they make this trip. Ensi found that it had been her plan from the beginning in hopes that such a visit would jar the talks loose.

*Nole agreed to this in an attempt to create a greater spirit of cooperation among the negotiators,* Ensi said.

"Yes, but from the look on Cieras's face, this may be another source of irritation," Iroshi replied. "She clearly believes this is totally unnecessary."

*As you suspect.*

"Drace seems to have mixed feelings about it all."

*She is a scientist. The only thing that interests her is going on with her work. All this negotiating and politicking interferes.*

"Does she have any sense of responsibility for what she creates and the effects it may have?"

*Not a bit. She leaves that in others' hands.*

"What are her feelings about the Patriarch?"

*He is a nuisance.*

"A woman after my own heart. At least in that respect."

She leaned against a stool. "What does she expect the role of her creation to be in the end?"

*Out of her control.* Iroshi started to say that was not an answer to her question, but Ensi went on hastily. *Any other feelings she may have are buried. She has worked as a scientist for several decades. She knows that once a product is developed she has no control. Except for moments like this, her current role in this project is to expand the research, to see if there are any other avenues to be explored: other uses, what other discoveries this one could lead to . . .*

"Side effects?"

*Trials have been made. How extensive I cannot say.*

". . . new formula is made exclusively from purely natural ingredients, plants grown right here on Djed," Drace was saying. "The only thing we do is the processing. It took some time to discover the right procedures and combinations of ingredients. Our world was settled nearly three hundred years ago; however, we're just beginning to explore all the possibilities inherent in its flora."

*That is because they first tried to kill off the native plants in order to grow well-known grains and other foodstuffs,* Ensi explained.

"What made you decide to experiment with such a formula, and why with these particular plants?" Iroshi asked.

"Random experimentation is a normal procedure," Drace said. "New medicines are being discovered all the time, based on the plants on so many worlds, most of which are totally wild. There are so many to choose from . . ." She shrugged.

"And the reason for researching such a formula?"

"One of those classic cases of looking for one thing and finding another."

"All right. Maybe you can tell me how your formula works."

"It's very complicated . . ."

"I am sure it is. Still, I can't believe that a simple explanation of the basics isn't possible."

Drace looked from Iroshi to Nole to Cieras, then back to Nole. The best guess would be that she had been told not to talk to Cieras about the details, and now she was on the spot.

*Quite right,* Ensi confirmed.

Iroshi folded her arms across her breasts, indicating that she was waiting and would not be put off by evasions. The doctor looked down at the notes in her hands as if the words she needed would be there.

"Essentially," she began without raising her eyes, "persea induces the body to initiate repairs more quickly. You see, as we grow older, our body gradually loses the ability to replace cells. The formula retards this loss."

She paused in hopes that enough had been said. However, everyone in the room remained quiet.

Instead of letting her off the hook, Iroshi asked, "Does it work on all body cells equally well?"

"Yes. That is one of the mysteries we haven't yet solved. It should probably work better on some than others. But that would take years of testing . . ."

"Never mind," Iroshi said. "I get the general idea. Is that all there is to see, then?"

"Well, here in the lab . . ."

"Not just here," Iroshi interrupted. "Where is the evidence that this anti-aging formula actually works? Did you experiment with animals? With people? Computer models?"

"A little of everything," Drace said. Her expression became gloomier, indicating that this was another line of information she was unwilling to pursue. "Unfortunately, live experimentation is still necessary as computer models cannot be programmed to take all possible variants into account. Every branch of science has found physical models to be quite necessary."

From across the room, one of Cieras's aides stared at Iroshi. Logan Rhiel was his name. The intensity of his gaze distracted her from what was being said. With a jolt she realized that the young man was displaying an interest beyond the professional. Not especially handsome, still he had an interesting face and a fine physique under the snug, navy blue jumpsuit, and why in the hell would he be interested in an eighty-seven-year-old woman? He could not be more than thirty-two.

Their eyes met and he smiled slightly. The old feelings rushed through her body and she struggled to listen to Drace, failed, wanted to give up. Several years had passed since Mitchell's death. As many men, or more, had visited her bed, or she theirs, but no permanent attachment had ever formed. At times, the absence of someone beside her in the night was unbearable. However, that had often been the case even when Mitchell lived, for they were separated so many times by the demands of her role within the Glaive.

Damn, where had all that come from? Just because a man looked at her, memories flooded in? Next she would be feeling the old guilt about not having children as Mitchell had wanted.

The young man looked away, releasing her attention back to the present. She sighed. Some old habits were hell to break.

Ensi filled her in on what had been said during the momentary lapse. Drace had just finished explaining how profound the results of the trials had been, although they had begun just less than nine years earlier. With the actual physical results, extended over fifty years by computer extrapolation . . .

"Well, the results were more astounding than we even

imagined," she continued. "Between the human trials and those with other mammals we import for the purpose, we estimate we can prolong human life for fifty to one hundred years."

She looked at Iroshi to gauge the effect. Disappointment clouded Drace's features for a moment, then disappeared. She should not have been surprised at a lack of reaction, since it was only logical that Erik would have explained all of this earlier.

"There really doesn't seem to be any reason for us to be here," Iroshi said to Ensi.

*I believe Drace's idea was simply to explain to the newest member of the negotiations what this matter is all about.*

"I can't help feeling she might have had more reason than that."

*Like what?*

"I don't know. I just don't know. She knows that she is telling me things that Erik would already have briefed me on. Except for the details about how persea works. Everyone else in here has seen it all. What the hell is it? What is she up to?"

*There is trouble outside,* Ensi said abruptly.

Erik stood straight, became more alert. He started edging closer to Iroshi, indicating with his eyes that she should move toward the back of the lab.

*A group of protestors is about to storm the building. Word will come soon from the guards outside.*

Erik took hold of her elbow and slowly guided her along between rows of workstations. Floyd and Jacob moved casually between them and the door. Drace's commentary faltered when she glanced in their direction. Iroshi pretended interest in something Erik was saying.

*Drace may know something about this.*

"I would not be surprised," Iroshi said. "What is this mob of people intending to do?"

*Few of the Djedians even know of persea's existence or what it does. These people appear to have been hired to disrupt our visit here. Since the lab is outside the city, few others will ever know this happened.*

He was working his way through numerous intellectual and emotional corridors among the supposed mob, trying to discover the common factor. Large groups of people could be more difficult to sift through than individuals. Iroshi kept silent, letting him wend his way to the facts they needed. Meanwhile, Drace droned on. She had moved to describing the functions of the different workstations within the lab.

*Everything is mixed together. I suspect that some of the mob think they are here for one reason, while they have actually been set in motion by someone else with a different agenda. There is a lot of thought along religious lines. However . . .*

The two Glaive representatives had reached the back of the lab. Drace had lost her audience, as everyone looked at the small group of Glaivers curiously. Iroshi held up her index finger, indicating that she needed a moment.

"Is there another door in here somewhere?" she whispered to Erik.

"I believe so," he answered. "Somewhere back here."

*I think I have found it.*

The main door banged open and a guard rushed into the room.

"Doctor Drace," he said as he rushed up to the scientist. "A mob has managed to make its way onto the grounds."

He went on to describe the circumstances outside the building: in spite of the security fence, about a hundred people were on the grounds and were at that moment marching on the research building. He did not think that the number of guards present could hold back the mob.

"Who are they?" Nole asked.

"They appear to be members of the temple. They are shouting things like, 'Don't play god,' and 'We all must die.'"

"Are they armed?"

"No, sir."

"Dammit, I knew those religious nuts would try to ruin my work," Drace said. "Nole, you've got to do something!"

"All right, Drace," Nole said. "Just calm down." He turned to the guard. "Call the Adjutant's office. Have them send a squad to keep this mob under control."

The guard started to leave, but Iroshi spoke up.

"Are you so sure these people intend to harm anyone?"

"Why else would they be here?" Drace demanded.

"There have already been some incidents," Nole said. "And, with so many important people gathered in this one room, I don't want to take any chances."

Within his mind there seemed to be a kind of pleasure in what was happening. Iroshi bowed her head in acceptance but continued.

"And what if we all left the room? Is there a back exit?"

Drace's face turned red and she spluttered a moment. "Of course, there is a back exit," she finally managed to say. "But why should we be forced to sneak out the back?"

"Why indeed?" Iroshi said. She spread her hands wide. "I leave the arrangements to you then, to protect these important people. For myself, however, I choose discretion."

She nodded to Erik. Placing his hand on the hilt of his sword, he led the way toward the hidden door both Ensi and Garon had detected.

*She does not want you to leave,* Ensi said. *I think she may have set this whole thing up.*

"Either she or Nole. She probably wants an incident that

will force Nole to destroy the temple or its influence. But Nole is either in on this little plan or it's helping his own plans in some way."

The door slid open when Erik pressed the control hidden under a shelf just beside it.

"I suspect the temple is at least as well organized as the government is," Iroshi finished as she started to follow through the opening. She turned a moment to appraise those standing silently in the lab. The young man grinned and saluted. She smiled back, returned the salute, then slipped into a narrow corridor. Her guards followed and closed the door, and everyone proceeded to the left. Before long the corridor opened into another, larger one.

"Do you know the way out?" Iroshi asked aloud.

"This way," Erik said, pointing right.

Clearly, he was following directions from Garon. Ensi was concentrating on events behind them and outside the building. The next hallway, larger still, was lit through windows along one whole wall. At the end, double doors.

"Those lead outside," Erik said.

"It's not far to our quarters, is it?"

"About ten miles."

She shrugged. "If the way is clear, why don't we just walk?"

"That's a long ways, Iroshi. That mob could be dangerous no matter who set them off. And in ten miles they could overtake us pretty easily," Erik said.

She looked at the guards behind. Jacob was scowling, clearly disapproving of this idea.

"Especially a woman of my age who can't walk very fast." Erik looked appropriately uncomfortable when she looked back at him. "If you get one of the cars," she continued, "they will hear and see us," she said. They had stopped just in front of the doors. "If we just walk away from the building, it will be between us and them. They won't know we're even outside until we are too far away for easy pursuit." She put her hand on the handle. "Besides, I haven't seen anything of the countryside or the city since I arrived. Only that short stretch between Godolphin House and here."

The three men looked at each other, first in consternation then in resignation. Except for Ensi, no one argued with her much anymore. Mitchell used to. All the time, lord love him, and always with her best interests at heart. Well, there were those rare meetings with Yail. When they first met he was so overawed by her that he never argued either. After several years as a constable, though, and rising in the ranks, he could give her a good argument without much hesitation. Having been her lover for a time, oh so long ago, he probably figured he had the right.

She pushed the door open and stepped out. The clear, sunny morning had turned cloudy and much colder. Walking might have been an unwise choice after all. Iroshi buttoned up her coat and pulled on the heavy gloves Erik had advised her to bring as she walked down the steps. Out of the corner of her eye she could see Erik wandering off at an angle. When she reached the bottom step she paused, turned in his direction, and watched. He strode up to a ground car and opened the door.

"Would you care to ride, madam?" he asked with a straight face.

She put both fists on her hips, tried to maintain a stern countenance, but it melted into a broad smile, then into laughter.

"You had this planned all along," she said, motioning toward the car.

"I wasn't taking any chances."

She climbed into the back seat while Floyd and Jacob took their places in the front. Erik walked around the vehicle and got in beside her. As she had suggested, Jacob steered a direct path away from the building, using it as a shield from the eyes of the mob.

"I had such a strange feeling about Drace's insistence that we come out here," he explained once they were on their way.

The road turned left, then Jacob increased the car's speed in case they were spotted. In spite of any possible danger, though, he drove leisurely once out of sight, taking a circuitous route back to the city to give her that look at the countryside, he said. The view was stark with strong hints of death. In early autumn, the colors promised renewal in the spring. Now, in late autumn, no promises were visible. How like Earth in its seasons and unlike Rune-Nevas, which strongly discouraged the people's efforts to make it look more like Earth. The image of one's home world always influenced humankind's vision of home. There were always differences no matter how hard they tried, some subtle, as here on Djed; some glaring, as on Rune-Nevas.

Then there was Rune-Nelson, once tamed by sentient life, but having reverted back to the wild millennia ago. Home to packs of carnivores and the animals that made up their prey, memories of it still brought chills. Where was home for her? Rune-Nevas? The logical place, since she lived there, spent most of her time there. And Mitchell was still there, if only in memory. Yet at least part of her heart remained on Earth, along with memories of Crowell, Mushimo, and her father. Rune-Nelson was a world she returned to over and over, both physically and in her mind, but never in her heart. Siebeling, the world of her birth, had never been home. It had only been familiar.

Djed reminded her too much of Earth, making her reflective and nostalgic. The people here were a strange lot. They were definitely unsophisticated at intrigue and negotiation, yet in most ways they had the upper hand in the current matter. So far, though, they seemed unsure as to how best to play that hand.

The Athenians, for all their experience, would continue to be frustrated, as difficult as that would have been to believe a few days ago. And the Glaive would fare no better unless they got a handle on things. It was beginning to seem that Djed might be regretting asking the Glaive for assistance. Particularly if Djedian aims had changed.

What *did* they want now? How did they intend going about getting it?

Damn! That was the worst part about unsophisticated groups. Their actions were unpredictable and their goals too simple to define.

*Trouble,* Ensi said.

"Where?"

*Just ahead.*

Jacob slowed the car on Erik's instructions; Garon had alerted him. The two guards unfastened their shoulder holsters. The pistols slid out with a soft sigh of plastic across cloth. Ensi said nothing else, meaning everyone was prepared. The road tunneled through a stand of trees.

*One hundred yards ahead, in the trees on the right. A large vehicle with several people. Six. They are going to block the road.*

Erik looked over at her questioningly.

"For what purpose?" she asked.

*Ostensibly to talk. They are armed and prepared for violence, however.*

"Who are they?"

Before Ensi could answer that one, a military-style vehicle burst out of the woods onto the road. It stopped directly in front of them, blocking their way.

Dukane paced the cabin with long, slow steps. Usually, waiting for something was easy—he simply did not think about it until it happened. However, this communication might rank as one of the most important of his life. It certainly would help decide the direction for the remainder of his career.

Vieren approached for the fourth time, stopping just short of his path. She looked up and whimpered when he passed, but he did not stop to soothe her with a pat on the head. His tension, which upset her, made him indifferent to her need for reassurance. Paige had tried to draw him into conversation, but he had brushed her off. Maybe if he concentrated hard enough, the damn comm would signal . . .

The comm alarm rang and he jumped, stopped, and wheeled toward the panel on the tiny writing desk. With a slightly shaking hand, he reached for the button to activate the screen. He hesitated. No need letting them know he was anxious.

They needed him more than he needed them.

He took a deep breath, which steadied his hand, and touched the button. Cline's face formed on the screen.

"He's on the comm," his pilot said.

"Yes," Dukane said. "Put him through."

Cline's plain features were replaced by another man's beautiful ones.

"Farlow, good to see you," Dukane said.

"I'm sure."

"What has been decided?" Was the question asked too eagerly?

Be more careful next time. He must control the situation. Deliberately, he pushed back in the chair, assuming a relaxed pose. Nothing must jeopardize this opportunity.

"We wish to accept your offer of assistance in this matter," Farlow said. "It is agreed that your knowledge and expertise should be of tremendous help. And, your price is quite reasonable."

Dukane would have helped them at no price at all, since

the purpose was to further his own aims. However, it was best not to give too much of an indication of his own agenda. As long as they did not ask directly, his purpose would remain secret.

"What you are trying to accomplish is a worthy cause," he said aloud.

Not a lie, after all, but not the entire truth. If no questions were asked, no more need be said.

"We believe it would be best to discuss strategy after your arrival," Farlow was saying. "Scrambled messages can only be so reliable."

"As you wish. I'll have Cline get the landing coordinates."

Farlow nodded. "We'll see you in three days, then."

Dukane signaled Cline. When he came on line, he instructed him to get the coordinates.

"And, Cline?" he continued.

"Yes?"

"Double-check them in the atlas. Just in case."

"Of course."

He tapped the transfer key, then disconnected. He now had a landing site unknown to Djedian officials. What would he have done if the temple officials had refused his help? Just landed on the planet and acted as he pleased anyway? That they would refuse had seemed a real possibility, given the length of time it had taken them to decide. Had there been time, he would have waited it out on Rune-Nelson, but each day he had remained brought the possibility of discovery ever closer.

Religious organizations were notoriously slow about making decisions, of course. They never wanted to give the impression of being in a hurry. They needed to make it seem as if the gods were consulted and that everyone gave the matter due consideration. Maybe even consult an oracle.

He would give them an oracle. And soon.

Looking down, he found Vieren settled on the floor just in front of him. He raised his feet and stretched out his legs over her. She cringed. Dumb animal. Didn't know a neutral gesture from a threatening one. He leaned over and patted her head. She pressed against his hand, making the near purring noise that showed booreecky contentment. Sandoval watched from across the room where he lay on his belly, legs folded under him.

"What's he thinking, Paige?"

The companion reached out, carrying Dukane with him. They touched the male's mind. Wildness in the animal flared a moment, then dimmed. Jealousy and fear mingled, then disappeared. The thing still resented Dukane and his dominance of Vieren. Maybe even his dominance of himself, too. The savage mind that had been the most difficult to control still wanted its freedom. However, it would never desert its mate. And she would always be tied closely to Dukane by the early bonding. Forever and ever, amen.

*Sandoval will kill you one day,* Paige said.

"Maybe. Or maybe I'll kill him before he has a chance."

*You enjoy baiting him too much. Life would not be nearly so much fun for you if he was gone.*

Dukane chuckled. She was right: tormenting Sandoval was even more fun than tormenting Vieren. How horrified the other Glaive members would be if they knew. He could just see them, wracking their brains. How could he have slipped through all their tests? What could they do with him now? He was a trained truthsayer, knowledgeable in their procedures, bound by their rules. But he knew how to play those rules for his own benefit while knowing how other truthsayers must act. It was like playing with children.

The same was true of the Djedians. No, even more so. Their lack of experience made them the perfect pawns in his own game. And they hadn't a clue.

Once more that train of thought carried Dukane along to the end. Iroshi and he should have been bonded all these years, but so many things had always been in the way. Mitchell was the biggest stumbling block, until he had finally died almost eight years earlier. Since that event, the time and circumstances never seemed right. The age difference was a consideration, as was his rather low position within the Glaive. He had never felt worthy of her attention, especially while she had remained celibate after losing her long-term companion. At least to all appearances that had been the case. Some within the Glaive had not believed that, given her reputation for lustiness.

His union with her was still desirable, might even have been possible as his work proceeded in the ruins of Rune-Nelson. His prestige had grown with the number of years. But Iroshi in little ways had shown she was not interested. Then, in a big way, she had rejected him when she took away his life's work. She must have been under a terrible strain to do that. However, it was clear she must be saved from herself. Why couldn't she see he only wanted what was best for her and the Glaive?

No use. The path was now inexorable. Their joining would be of a different kind. More complete. Closer. Even more satisfying.

# 7

✦✦

Two men stepped out of the vehicle and stood beside it. They wore green military jumpsuits and jackets, and combat boots. Dark goggles partially hid their faces, but they wore no hats. The one on the left was dark blond; the other had medium brown hair. The blond crossed his arms over his chest; the other placed his hands on his hips. Both watched the car.

"How shall we handle it?" Erik asked.

"Let them wait," Iroshi said, "while Ensi and Garon glean as much information as they can."

"Shall *we* see what they want?" Jacob asked from the driver's seat, unaware of her conversation with Ensi.

"Not yet," she said. "I want to know what these people want and if these are leaders or soldiers first."

"Couldn't we just back out of here?" he asked.

He would always prefer action to contemplation, unlike Floyd. Their differences in character balanced the team, making them the types of guards she liked having around.

"That wouldn't accomplish much and might not be necessary," she said. "They're not exactly threatening us yet."

*They carry several kinds of weapons,* Ensi said. *But no guns.*

Djed was essentially free of guns—wild game for hunting was almost nonexistent, and such weapons were forbidden by law for any other use. That law had been written and pushed by the temple and its leaders. There had been little gunrunning; what smuggler would look for business on a third world where the payoff would be slim at best? As with any society forbidden one kind of weapon, many of the Djedians had turned to martial arts and the weapons those disciplines espoused as a sort of retaliation. All of that—the state religion's influence, the reliance on martial arts, and their third-world status—were the reasons she had agreed to take the Djedians on as pro bono clients. She did not plan to regret that decision.

*The list of players grows,* Ensi said. *These people represent a group that has no objections to persea and what it does, unlike the religious right. They would much prefer, however, that neither the Athenians nor the Glaive had anything to do with it. They see it as a purely Djedian product that should be entirely controlled by their own people without outside interference.*

"Do they have a plan for marketing it?"

*Oh, they have doubts about marketing it at all outside of Djed. They think it might not only be possible, but also desirable to keep it all to themselves. That might be the edge they need to raise their position and thumb their noses at the rest of us.*

"Not very farsighted," Iroshi commented. "Any connection to the Patriarch?"

*None.*

Iroshi sighed. "A nationalist group, then. I think this whole affair is becoming overly complicated."

*Agreed,* Ensi said.

"It is," Erik said.

The two men confronting the car continued to wait.

"Are they merely soldiers?" Iroshi asked.

*No. Their leadership has become a little complicated of late, however, and these two at least receive guidance from someone else. Whoever that might be waits to see what happens here.*

"Erik," she said aloud. "Go tell them we do not discuss important matters in the middle of the road. If their leaders want to talk with me, they can make an appointment."

Erik nodded and started to open the door.

"Floyd, go with him," she said.

They stepped out and walked ahead of the car. Once they stood face-to-face with the pseudo military men, Erik talked and the two Djedians listened. Then the strangers became animated. The one on the right argued, as Ensi reported, that they would not be ordered around by some Glaiver. His arms and hands gesticulated wildly, accenting his words. The blond grabbed his compatriot's arm, trying to calm him, although he, too, appeared angry. The latter fact was confirmed by Ensi.

The darker-headed man placed his hands back on his hips, but said no more. Erik reiterated his statement, the blond nodded, and Erik and Floyd returned to the car.

"Watch them, Ensi," Iroshi said.

The warning was probably unnecessary, but the attitude of the Djedians was now so clearly belligerent, even from a distance, that she expected the worst. However, Erik and Floyd made it back to the car without incident. As they got in, the larger vehicle backed off the road, the two men walking alongside it, never taking their eyes off the car.

"These people are looking for a fight," Erik said as Jacob started the car. "I gathered that their whole aim is to keep Djed out of the clutches of other powers, a definite isolationist agenda. They did say that they'll be in touch."

Jacob started the car forward. They were watched until the car disappeared from sight around a bend in the road. The tunnel of trees continued a mile after that, ending abruptly with clear fields on either side of the road. The capital city sat ahead, its perimeter totally clear of trees or any plants other than grass, as if to prevent anyone from sneaking up on it. The tallest building was thirteen stories—rather, there were two of them. Several only slightly shorter were scattered along the skyline. Provincial compared to many capital cities. Rather larger than any on Rune-Nevas, where she had deliberately worked to keep the population low and largely dependent on the Glaive for a living.

One thing she missed, Iroshi decided, was air cars. Although the experience of driving along the ground was bringing back some memories of her first trip to Earth, she did not recall such travel being quite so rough. Well, she had been younger then. She shifted in her seat to break the train of thought.

What a waste of time the day had been. The visit to the lab had produced no useful information. Well, that was not entirely true. Those who wanted the Glaive's help had shown they would do almost anything to ruin the reputation of the religious group. The last group—or she hoped the last of them—had adopted a paramilitary stance to put their isolationism forward. Amateurs all. Dangerous too.

"Do you remember the name of the young man in Cieras's group today?" she asked suddenly.

"Which one?" Erik asked.

"The blond in the . . ."

". . . grey suit," Erik finished.

*When will you ever learn?* Ensi admonished.

"Look," she said. "Don't go getting the wrong idea."

"I saw him looking at you."

"And maybe we can use his interest to support our own."

"What is our interest, anyway?"

She started to answer sharply but realized the question was a valid one. They seemed to have lost sight of what their interest was here on Djed. Or their purpose. All of a sudden they were at odds with all factions here over something no one would talk about honestly. Then there was the mystery of the woman with no soul or mind.

They entered the precincts of the city. On the outskirts,

as with so many towns and cities, the capital began with run-down houses and ill-repaired streets. Except for the main road on which they drove, of course.

"We were invited here to help the Djedians in their negotiations with the Athenians," she said. Erik nodded. "I don't see that our purpose has changed. However, until these people are honest with us about this persea and its effects and side effects, we cannot do our job."

"So, now we start looking into the research . . ."

"Everything having to do with persea. The plants they use. How they process them. And what the hell that strange woman has to do with any of this."

"You mean Prilly Jaxe?" Erik said. "Do you really think she has something to do with all this?"

"Not as an active participant, but somehow, some way. She didn't just happen to wander into Godolphin House."

"I didn't think she did, but what role could she possibly play?"

"I think she was used to test persea."

Questions sprang from Erik and the two companions as the car neared Godolphin House. She let them go on until Jacob had the car parked. Absently, she noted that the Athenians' car was not parked at the guest house next door.

"All right," she said, holding up her left hand. "You talk like you hadn't guessed the same thing. I know it occurred to you. My guess would be, Erik, that the formula is what turned her into a zombie. Maybe she wasn't in her right mind at the time it was given to her. Whatever the details are, it's the only possible reason for someone wanting us to see her."

"Well, yes, the possibilities had occurred to me," Erik said. "But there is another one. Given her resemblance to Nole's wife, couldn't someone have hoped to cause him embarrassment through her?"

"Perhaps," she said.

Iroshi opened her door and stepped out. The sky had darkened even more during the ride back, and the storm would break soon. A wind blew fresh and chill, and she shivered. For a moment, when autumn first made itself evident, there had been wisps of longing for the season that never appeared on Rune-Nevas. That longing disappeared with the wind. It was very sharp, smelled of impending snow, and blew in strong gusts as they walked up the steps of the house. All thought of conversation also disappeared until she and Erik were settled within the confines of the master suite.

"All right," Iroshi began as they settled into chairs. "Back to what you said about Jaxe, Erik. It seems clear that embarrassing Nole was one of the aims of the people who sent her to us. However, I don't think she just looked like Nole's wife. I think she *was* Nole's wife."

"What?" Erik said rather too loudly. "I just saw her, well, not long ago. She was ill, but nothing like what we saw here."

"Was the illness a fatal one?" she asked.

"I understood that it could be. But no announcement has been made as to what the illness was or that she's gotten worse."

"But, it's been two or three weeks since you saw her?"

"Yes, at least that."

"What if Drace figured that, if her formula would prolong life, it might cure whatever illness Mrs. Nole had? But it had the opposite effect instead. Such a blunder could make the Djedians think twice about their formula. Worse, it could make the Athenians think twice."

"They would want to keep problems quiet, that's true," Erik agreed.

He leaned back in his chair in deep thought for a moment. Sounds of lunch preparation crept softly upward, through the corridors and walls, from the kitchen. Iroshi studied her surroundings, clearing momentarily her mind of the current problems for a moment. She liked the size of their house and its isolation from the palace. Since Djed had relatively few official or state visitors, houses had been built and furnished only along one street for such contingents. Even though Victorian in style, Godolphin House was more plainly decorated compared to the palace. Something to be grateful for.

"All right," Erik said at last. "If she is Mrs. Nole, and persea had such an effect on her, for whatever reason, they would want to keep that very quiet. What we don't know is why the formula would have such an effect and why or when it was given to her."

"The one thing we must confirm," Iroshi interrupted, "is whether the woman actually is Mrs. Nole. Can Garon search for her? He knows her mind pattern better than Ensi does and would have a better chance of finding her."

After a very short pause, Erik nodded. "He is starting now."

A bell sounded, announcing lunch. They started down.

"His name is Logan Rhiel," Erik said suddenly.

"Who?"

"Cieras's aide."

"Thank you."

Entering the dining room, they found Floyd and Jacob waiting. While the conversation had continued upstairs, the two guards had swept the house for listening devices and anything else that might be unwelcome. They took no chances in spite of the house having been occupied the whole time by the cook and steward. The four took seats around the table, and Harleq entered a few minutes later with the cart. In a very few minutes he had served everyone, placed the serving dishes on the sideboard, and returned to the kitchen.

Formal eating was a pleasure Iroshi indulged in when

traveling. However, by the time she returned home, she'd had her fill and went back to her habit of eating off a tray in front of the computer, or at her desk. That had become her habit ever since Mitchell died, leaving her to dine alone much of the time. Gods! she missed him still. Nothing seemed to dim the sense of loss—not time, or short-term affairs, or work. Nothing.

*If he had only let us teach him,* Ensi said.

"I know," she said silently. "He never wanted the knowledge. Never liked the idea of other spirits sharing his body, or his sharing someone else's body. He was content as he was."

She looked at the food on the fork hovering just above the plate. It had lost its appeal, but she must eat something. One nice thing about being head of the Glaive and the rich lifestyle it made possible—she never had to settle for artificials. Real food was taken everywhere she went, even provided for any Glaive members who preferred it. Not all did, depending on where and how they had grown up.

The door chimed, rousing her from useless contemplation. Harleq's footsteps could be heard in the main hall. Jacob and Floyd pushed back their chairs and stood. In a moment, the dining room door closed on Jacob as he left the room, and Floyd moved to stand just inside the door. She took a bite of food as Ensi checked out the visitor.

*Someone from the Athenian delegation,* Ensi finally announced. *Very excited.*

In another moment, Harleq escorted a gentleman in. She recalled his name as Simon Terrell, one of Cieras's aides.

"There's been an attempt on Lenora Cieras's life," he said breathlessly.

Clearly this was a totally unexpected event to him.

"Is she all right?" Iroshi asked, real concern edging her voice.

"Yes. She was slightly wounded. They shot at us from

the woods. She suffered a flesh wound on her right hand. If it hadn't been for the Djedian guards that were accompanying us back here, it might have been much worse."

"A shot?" Then someone did have a gun or two. "It wasn't a result of the demonstration outside the lab?"

She looked at Erik, then back at Terrell, who shook his head.

"Please, Mr. Terrell, take a seat," she went on. "Harleq, get Mr. Terrell a glass of wine."

The man collapsed into the nearest chair with a breathless "Thank you." No one spoke while Harleq poured the wine at the sideboard, then carried it to the table. Terrell took a sip.

"Thank you," he said again. "I apologize for the intrusion. We wanted you to be aware of this treachery immediately." He swallowed more of the wine.

"We were accosted on the road coming back. Nine ruffians, all masked. I think the presence of the extra guards surprised them. We were unarmed, of course. Business just isn't done that way."

"No, indeed," Iroshi said. "Have you any idea who the attackers may have been?

"None. You may want to send a request to Guien Nole for additional guards here, too. No telling what these people might do." He downed the last of the wine. "I must get back," he said as he rose from the chair. "Thank you for the wine. It helped immensely."

"You're welcome," Iroshi said. "Let us know if anything else happens."

"I will," Terrell said. He bowed, then followed Harleq out.

Jacob returned and shut the door. Neither he nor Floyd resumed their seats immediately. Tensed for action, they preferred to relax gradually just in case something further should occur.

"Another threat from the same people we encountered?" Iroshi asked after a short silence.

"It doesn't seem likely," Erik replied. "They didn't attack us, after all. They weren't even prepared to talk at the time, much less fight."

"Oh, I think they were more prepared to fight than anything." She turned inward. "Ensi, you said the leader may have been nearby. Could he or she have sent the ones who attacked the Athenians?"

*Possibly. I never got a clear image of anyone other than those we faced.*

A few minutes later, an explosion rocked the house. The windows rattled. Voices began screaming.

# 8

❖

Cold, stinging mist slapped her in the face. She gasped, swallowed a great lungful of smoke. Her throat burned, tears ran down her cheeks, froze there, and she stumbled down the steps. Jacob, near at hand as always, caught her arms, eased her to the ground, and set her down. The latter was roughly done, and he immediately began apologizing.

Unable to speak yet, Iroshi placed a hand on his arm in reassurance. If it hadn't been for him, she would have fallen face first down the steps. A few feet ahead, Erik and Floyd ran on toward the Athenian house, having assured themselves that she was safe in Jacob's hands. Literally.

"I'm all right," she said huskily. She pulled the hood of her coat over her head and breathed into the fabric, warming her lungs, nose, and mouth.

She tried to get him to follow the others, but he would not go. One of the three would be at her side at all times, and the lot had fallen to him. A comforting thought. But the failure of her own body was a betrayal she could scarcely bear. Having witnesses only made the frustration worse.

Carefully she stood, with his help, and stepped forward. In spite of the cold and the mist frozen in her hair, the ground was not yet slick with ice. Clearly, the cold had come on too suddenly for the ground to freeze. The wind, however, had cooled her skin enough for the moisture to freeze on her face.

Stepping gingerly, she moved toward the scene of confusion. Smoke rolled from windows, the mirglass broken or badly cracked. Shouts came from inside and out. She would almost guess that Jacob saw none of it, so intent was he on watching her.

*I do not think there is any real danger,* Ensi said softly. *In spite of all the noise.*

"Why? What is it?"

*Some sort of minor, if noisy, accident. Cieras is coming out now.*

The head of the Athenian delegation appeared in the doorway, coughing and rubbing her eyes. She started toward Erik, spotted Iroshi, and waved. After speaking to Erik a moment, she met Iroshi halfway between the houses.

"Sorry about all the fuss," Cieras said. "We were holding a small ceremony in thanks for our safe delivery this afternoon. Our damned brazier blew up. More bang and smoke than anything, although Terrell was burned a bit."

"Do you have a doctor?" Iroshi asked.

"Yes, thank you. He's being seen to on the other side of the house. It will be a few hours before anyone will be able to breathe inside."

"You're welcome to stay in Godolphin House tonight, while yours is cleared," Iroshi said, waving away the smoke that kept drifting into her face.

"Thank you, but I should oversee the cleanup."

"Nonsense. There are more than enough people to take care of it." Iroshi motioned toward the small crowd gathered outside the still smoking house. "Have whatever papers you might need gathered up and brought over. We'll set you up in one of the upstairs bedrooms."

"Are you sure it won't be inconvenient?"

"Of course."

While Cieras went off to make arrangements for the move, Erik approached Iroshi with a somber look.

"Are you sure this is a good idea?" he asked. "The Djedians might see it as a betrayal."

"Then they will have to move very fast to repair the house or arrange new quarters for the Athenians, won't they?" She pulled the hood of her coat closer around her face. "Contact Nole," she continued. "Tell him what's happened. Make it sound . . . oh, conspiratorial. Between him and me."

"You're stirring things up."

"Has it ever seemed odd to you that both worlds involved in this deal have based their civilizations on ancient Earth cultures? Even the names: Djed and Athens."

"I never thought about it." Erik looked puzzled.

"Oh, it doesn't mean anything really. Just an odd coincidence, I guess."

*If it means nothing, why did you bring it up?*

"Just thinking aloud," she answered silently. "Don't you think it odd?"

The next hour saw a flurry of activity. Cieras and her staff moved boxes into the large bedroom in the upper right corner. Erik excused himself to contact Nole. Since Floyd and Jacob slept at different times, they were put together in the smaller room with two beds, and Erik moved into the third room. Although the room was swept daily, Iroshi had Floyd and Jacob make absolutely sure there were no listening devices or cameras in Cieras's room.

The wind howled around the corners of the house as Iroshi and Erik at last settled into her sitting room. Harleq had reheated the food and insisted they finish their meal like civilized people, although it was now dinnertime rather than lunchtime. Cieras and her aide had politely refused to join them, preferring to have something brought over from their own kitchen and eating in their room. Finding a small bed had proved difficult, but one of the Djedian soldiers had managed it somehow. It was placed in the room for the aide.

"Now I know why you invited her to stay," Erik said innocently.

"Why do you think?"

"You knew she would bring Logan Rhiel with her. I saw the look the two of you exchanged when he came into the house."

"Don't be impertinent. How would I have known she would choose to bring him rather than someone else?"

Actually, it had been just a stroke of luck for all she knew, and she found it difficult to squelch a grin. Whether it was good luck or bad was yet to be determined.

She stretched, working out a few kinks in her arms and shoulders. No one had mentioned her collapse as they all rushed from the house, something she was grateful for. It would not have happened when she was younger—at least she did not think so. Although the combination of frigid air and smoke could have such an effect on even a younger person.

"It's been a long day," she said, as she settled back into the cushions.

"A strange day," Erik corrected.

"Yes, very strange. Even worse, nothing that happened has gotten us any nearer to the truth of what's going on."

"True. Except this new group we have to consider. They're dangerous, but I don't think they'll be much of a factor in the negotiations."

"If we ever get back to the table again."

"We will," Erik reassured her. "I know it hasn't seemed like it, but the Djedians really want to become a power in the empire. They are tired of being a backwater world."

"Would they lie about persea and its aftereffects to gain that new respect?"

Erik took a sip of his tea, a new blend Iroshi had brought with her. Having others in the house did not exactly preclude drinking wine; however, it was safer not to indulge. Erik probably regretted that. He had developed a real liking for that local red wine. Not that he overindulged. She would know if that was the case.

Or would she? The failure to detect Dukane had damaged her belief in her ability to read people and her belief in the selection process. If Dukane could get into the Glaive, and his aberrations go undetected for so many years, there was a definite problem.

But there were no problems with Erik. She had known him too long and too well to think otherwise.

*Be sure in that knowledge,* Ensi said. Before she could respond, Erik continued.

"I don't believe they would lie about the formula itself. I think it does exactly what they say it will do. They might lie about side effects. That's what you're thinking, isn't it?"

Iroshi nodded.

"All right. If it turned Mrs. Nole into a zombie, why doesn't she look the same? There is a strong resemblance between her and Jaxe, but it's not exact."

"The face of Mrs. Nole that you saw before had life in it. Expression. Prilly Jaxe's did not. Her lack of expression was like a dead person's."

Erik finished the tea as he considered what she said.

"Then we must confirm your suspicions about that. The best way may be to search discreetly for Mrs. Nole."

"Garon has had no luck with that?" Erik shook his head. "Keep at it," she said. She stood and stretched again. "It's late. I'm going downstairs and look for a book to read."

"A book?"

"Yes, you remember. Pages between covers with words printed on them."

She went to the door of the suite.

"I've seen one or two," he said, looking perplexed. "However, there are none in the house; particularly, there are none downstairs."

Clearly Erik was not into reading the reprints of old romances and did not get the oblique reference. Iroshi had picked one up on her last visit to Earth. Silly stuff, but originally written when the heroine did go downstairs for a book, only to run into the hero.

"I'll get a cup of hot chocolate, then."

"You hate chocolate."

She shrugged and laughed, then opened the door.

"Maybe something else will present itself."

Erik shook his head and smiled.

"Your libido will be the death of you one of these days," he said.

"Not a bad way to go. Goodnight."

"'Night."

Jacob nodded as she passed. Without a word or a sound, he followed. She could feel his presence even if he was hard to see in the darkened stairway. She paused at the bottom of the stairs. What was it she had expected to find, anyway? It would be nice to think that Logan might be having the same thoughts as she was, but not likely. Jacob would know where he was, but it was not really important enough to ask. The little jaunt was as much to get the feel of the house as it sat still and quiet for the night.

She walked into the sitting room, went over to the large window looking out onto the front lawn. The grass now sparkled with a sheen of ice. Apparently, the ground had gotten cold enough for the mist to freeze after all. The first moon, sitting near the horizon, set the tips of the icy blades aglow and cast short, narrow shadows in the opposite direction. The overall effect was a mottled landscape, seeming in miniature.

The air itself shimmered as the mist now fell in ice droplets, each backlit by the moon. Iroshi pressed her fingertips lightly against the window. In spite of the insulation properties of the mirglass, it was very cold to the touch. If this was autumn, what could winter be like?

"Hey!"

The shout came from behind her. She spun and crouched,

reaching for the sword that lay on the dresser in her bedroom instead of being slung across her back. In shadows near the door, two men struggled. Moonlight caught a head of blond hair and set it alight. A nearly bald pate glowed nearly as much.

"It's all right, Jacob," Iroshi said firmly. "Logan Rhiel means me no harm."

"Damned right," the same voice said, sounding a little strained.

"As you say, Iroshi," Jacob said.

A harsh rustle of clothes brushing against each other told her the hold had been released. Jacob's shadowy figure left the room but stayed within sight in the hall.

"I did not mean to disturb you, Iroshi," Logan said. "I was feeling a little tight after the day's excitement. If I had my equipment, I could work out the tension, but everything is back in the other house."

His was a very nice voice, masculine but with little hardness to it.

"What kind of workout do you do?"

"Martial arts. A mixture of techniques. Some weight training. Meditation. Actually, I was trying to find a secluded spot for practice and maybe a little meditation when your guard caught me."

"You can use the conference room if you like."

She tried to look back at the scene on the other side of the window, but looking into the eyes of the young man before her was so pleasing. Especially when they showed his interest so clearly. This might be a foolish game to play, but life was to be enjoyed.

"Thank you," Logan said, and she realized they had been staring at each other for the space of several heartbeats. "It's beautiful, isn't it?" He motioned toward the window.

"Yes, it is." She finally turned to look out. "We don't have weather like that on Rune-Nevas."

"We do sometimes on Athens."

He drew closer to get a better view of the icy scene. His warmth embraced the length of her arm, contrasting sharply with the chill the view induced. It was a nice feeling, being close to a man to whom she was attracted. The realization seeped in that she was not sure how far she was prepared to go with this one. Casual affairs had lost their charm in recent years. That had made for many lonely nights. She still did not like sleeping alone.

Now she was really getting ahead of herself. He might find her interesting, but that did not mean he wanted to make love to her, in any sense of the term.

She cut her eyes to look at him. Yes, he did want to. Or thought he did. Had he ever made love to a woman in her eighties?

"Hmm," he said suddenly. "This is mesmerizing. If I'm going to practice, I had better get to it."

"Yes. Well, I'll tell Jacob you will be in the conference room."

"Thank you."

Logan held out his hand, and she took it in her own. It was so warm against her skin. She looked into his eyes, drawn into their depths. Too dark to tell if they were blue or brown or whatever color they might be. His Adam's apple bobbed as he swallowed.

"Goodnight," he said, but made no effort to remove his hand.

"Goodnight. Enjoy your practice."

"Could I . . . No. Never mind."

"What?" she asked.

"It would be too forward to ask."

This was the beginning of games, and she hated games.

*He is in awe of you,* Ensi said suddenly. *His hesitation is genuine.*

She nearly jumped in surprise. Ensi usually did not take

any interest in her romances, except to give her a hard time every once in a while.

"Don't beat around the bush, Mr. Rhiel." She freed her hand.

He smiled.

"All right. I was wondering if I could come by your suite for a talk after I've finished my workout."

"About anything in particular?"

"No, nothing in particular." His smile broadened.

"There's a good chance I'll still be up another couple of hours. I have a lot of work to do. Ask Jacob to check when you come upstairs."

"I will. And thank you again."

"You're welcome."

Iroshi turned and left the room. She knew his eyes followed her as she walked across the entry hall and up the stairs. A new exhilaration and alertness lightened her step. Nothing like a bit of flirtation to liven one's day.

At her door, she told Jacob where Logan would be then went inside. Once in the suite, she looked at the desk with distaste. She had not been lying when she talked of work. Message cubes were stacked on the desk, report cubes beside them, and correspondence beside them. All had been screened by Erik and marked for level of importance. She had always taken pride in looking over all reports coming in from the field and reviewing all requests for Glaive assistance. However, as more and more members were available to go into the field, and more and more requests came in, giving personal attention to only special cases was becoming more and more attractive and probably necessary.

Mitchell had always urged her to do so, even when the workload had been less. Not that he took his own advice. He had worked harder than anyone in the Glaive. It had pleased him to do so. And when death approached too closely, he had refused her offer of near immortality.

"I worked hard enough in this life," he said. "One is all I need."

He was almost a hundred when his artificial heart gave out. The doctors said implanting another one just would not work.

This was a hell of a time to remember all of that, she thought, wiping a tear from her eye. After all this time, she should have gotten more at ease with the memories, but maybe she never would. They had been together a long time, she and Mitchell. And they had stayed very much in love in spite of their other affairs. Well, mostly *her* other affairs. But he had never asked her to be faithful, and he certainly would not ask it of her now.

Gods, she must be getting old. A maudlin old fool.

*Not quite.*

"Oh, hush, Ensi."

*You are going to do it again?*

"What? Have an affair?"

*Yes.*

"If the spirit is willing, I am."

Ensi chuckled.

*I cannot say that living inside you has ever been boring.*

"I'm glad to hear that. I would be so sad if I had ever bored you."

He chuckled again.

*There are some important matters among the report cubes,* he said, changing the subject. *Will you look at them now?*

"Not yet. I want to practice first. Then I'll look at them."

She changed clothes, then went to the dresser where all of her swords lay. She touched the katana lovingly. It was more than a thousand years old, but the handle still looked as if it were brand-new. Picking it up, she slid the blade partway out. It reflected light like a mirror. Not a trace of the blood that had coated it so many times. She shoved the blade back and picked up the bamboo shinai. Sometimes she practiced with the short wakizashi, but most times of late she preferred the lighter shinai. It did not tire her quite so much. Another sign of getting older?

Yes or no, it did not matter. The journey to death was inexorable and, for her, nothing to be feared. No member of the Glaive would ever die, except in those rare accidents that happened too unexpectedly.

She activated the spar, and soon the bamboo shaft cracked against the laser shaft. Before each lunge, each swing of the shinai, her kiai filled the room, becoming part of the action. Half an hour passed. Her skin glistened with sweat, and her limbs and body felt warm and loose. She turned off the spar with the remote strapped to her wrist and grabbed a towel. None of the laser bursts had touched her; good to know she was still fast enough to defend herself. Although that had been proved back on Rune-Nelson, had it not?

She shed the soaked jumpsuit and stepped into the shower. In a few minutes she was clean and dry and wearing clean clothes. The report cubes still waited, and she took the one on top and inserted it into the reader.

When a knock came on the door, she looked up at the clock. Half an hour had passed, and half of the first cube was read and the reports noted. Iroshi stood and stretched. Was it Logan at the door? Who else would it be at this time of night?

*It is Logan. I believe he also showered after practicing.*

"I'm certainly glad of that."

She went to the door and opened it. The young man stood there, trying not to look at Jacob, who stood to the right looking at nothing.

"Come in," Iroshi said. She stood to one side, then closed the door behind him. "Have a seat."

"Thanks."

Logan moved to the sofa and sat at one end. As he had entered, she had noticed that his eyes were chocolate brown.

"Something to drink?"

"Sure. Whatever you're having."

"Just some hot tea," she said.

"That's fine."

She brought the two cups to the sofa. For a while they compared reactions to Djed. He found it a little more backward than most of the worlds he had been assigned to in the past, but not intolerable. Although they lacked a few of the amenities available on most of the more progressive worlds, the Djedians themselves were not quite as jaded.

"Persea will certainly change all of that once it's marketed," Iroshi said. "One can only wonder how such a backward world managed to create such a thing."

"As Doctor Drace said, they found it more by accident and luck than anything," Logan said. "Like most really important scientific discoveries. It could make Djed very important. The main component is, after all, a native plant. I understand that some plants cannot be grown anywhere other than in their native soil."

"Someone has tried to grow these elsewhere?"

"Not that I know of. But someone will, eventually."

"You seem to know more about it than anyone except the Djedians."

"Yes. Well." He nearly blushed. "Senta Drace has taken a sort of interest in me." He cleared his throat. "That is, we've had dinner together several times and she talked to me about her discovery. She is quite proud of her work."

"Is he here to tell me what he knows?" Iroshi asked Ensi silently.

*It does not seem so. However, I will delve a little deeper for his motives.*

"Are the two of you seeing each other?"

"Only occasionally." Logan pressed his left temple with his fingertips. "I'm afraid that most of the interest is on her side. Cieras encourages her to invite me over for dinner, and we've gone out to concerts and things a few times."

He frowned and went silent a moment.

"Please, Iroshi. Get out of my mind."

# 9

✧

"Ensi, back off!"

*I am out. I had no idea.*

"I'm sorry, Logan," Iroshi said aloud. "I don't know what you mean."

"Oh, it wasn't you, was it?" He looked confused; then his expression changed to one of understanding. "It was someone very close to you. Someone who is a part of you."

"I don't understand." She put as much confusion and sincerity into her voice as she could muster.

"Of course," Logan continued, as if he had not heard her. "It would be a secret. It would also explain many things."

"Logan, I don't understand what you are talking about," she said with greater emphasis.

"Please, Iroshi. You know exactly what I am talking about. I only wish I knew more." He sat back, relaxed, a look of fascination now on his face. "I only got a glimpse of you."

"Are you telling me that you're psychic?"

"No, I'm telepathic. No one knows that. Except you, of course."

"Only because you just told me."

"You didn't know before?"

"No," she admitted. "Why didn't we know?" she asked Ensi silently.

*He is very good at hiding his talent. In all our years we*

*have never come across anyone quite like him, with more natural abilities and discipline.*

Logan looked over at her quizzically.

"Can he pick up anything we're saying now?"

*No. However, I think he is suspicious.*

"Damn, we've always been so careful before." Aloud, she said, "What are you thinking?"

"True telepaths are very rare. I've never met another one myself. Have you? I mean, you are older than I am and have traveled even more. I just thought if anyone had met others, it must be you."

"Is that why you came here tonight? To ask me that?"

"Of course not. I came to see you. To get to know you. I really wanted that. I still do."

She reached over and patted his hand where it rested on a cushion between them. "Maybe another time," she said. "What just happened has been a little disturbing."

"I am sorry," he said. "I probably shouldn't have said anything, but it was the first time I ever felt someone else's presence inside my mind. It was unnerving."

"But what if it wasn't me? What if it was someone trying to make you think it was me?"

"I could . . . taste you. I know that doesn't make much sense. But that's the only way I can describe how it felt. It was only when I realized that I could feel someone else at the same time that I knew you did not come alone.

"I won't tell anyone, you know. About the telepathy thing."

"Why not? If what you're thinking is true, wouldn't it be of immense use to Cieras and her mission here? It might even get you a promotion."

Logan grinned for the first time. His teeth were slightly crooked, surprising since he could clearly afford the latest in cosmetic perfection. But the flaw did give him a devil-may-care look, which might be the objective, after all.

"First, I have no doubt that you would kill me," he said. "Or have me killed, if you believed it was important enough to keep this secret. Second, what I or Cieras might gain would not be worth the price it would cost you. I'm not even sure we would gain anything. No one has ever managed to blackmail a Glaive member to my knowledge. Your reputation for honesty would probably keep anyone from believing me—or most people, anyway."

He paused again, looked her full in the face, then continued.

"Last, I would have to admit that I am telepathic, and I won't do that."

*There is some personal experience he is afraid to tell,* Ensi said. *I do not know if the memory itself frightens him, or if he fears letting someone else know what happened.*

"Stay out," Iroshi told Ensi.

*It was something I caught before,* he said petulantly, then withdrew.

"Let me just say that Athenians are not tolerant of people who are different," Logan said after a very long pause.

She apologized to Ensi, but did not know if her companion heard. He had always been a little testy about criticism, but it seemed to be getting worse. Or was it the incidences of criticism that were getting worse? Maybe she was the one getting testy.

Silence lengthened both within and without. Iroshi relaxed against the sofa, prepared to wait for the others to speak first.

"I hope I haven't offended," Logan said at last.

"There has been no offense," Iroshi said.

Saying nothing further regarding his accusation must equal admission in his mind. However, if she protested ignorance, that might also lend credence to his words. Neither denial nor confirmation was best. His sensitivity clearly meant that he would not be convinced otherwise, anyway.

His words had revealed a certain sympathy with her or the Glaive. Or was it antipathy toward his own cause? Either way, there might be an alliance in the making.

"Perhaps I should leave," Logan said suddenly, but he made no move to rise.

Her silence had made him uneasy.

"I'm sorry," she apologized. "As I said, there is no offense. I was just deep in thought. So much has happened today."

He repeated his offer to leave, and she demurred. It was getting late, but he did not really seem to want to go. Nor did she want him to. For her, he was a different type of person than she was accustomed to. Most of the true telepaths she knew were members of the Glaive. However, they had joined while they were children, and their talents had been nurtured within the guild. Oh, there had been one or two outsiders, but they had never figured prominently in Glaive business. Logan was worth knowing, and she asked questions about his life.

His parents had been ambassadors, traveling from minor world to minor world through rotating assignments. Although they never said so, he suspected they did not return home often because of his talent for telepathy. Strangeness in people from another world was acceptable; strangeness in your next-door neighbor was not. That was one of the reasons he had chosen to work as an economic liaison specializing in off-world negotiations. Then he backed up and gave her the vital statistics. He was thirty-eight years old, never married, although bonded for five years with a woman who worked as liaison on one of the worlds he had been assigned to. There were no children. He made a good living and . . .

He stopped, looked at Iroshi with some embarrassment, and would not continue no matter what she said.

"That last thought somehow involved me, didn't it?" she asked finally.

His grin made him look younger. It faded quickly, as if he had mentally reminded himself that coyness was a child's game and he was a grown-up.

"You were going to tell me how you're always attracted to older women. Right?"

Logan's hand automatically went to his forehead. "You didn't . . ." he began.

"No, no," she reassured him. "It just seemed the logical progression for some reason."

"You've been told that before, I'll bet."

"A couple of times."

"Sorry to be so common." He jumped to his feet. "I really do have to go now."

"Please, Logan. Don't be embarrassed. A lot of young men are fascinated by older women. For many different reasons."

"But I . . ." he began. "It's getting late."

"Sit, down," she urged. "We can talk a little longer. I did want to ask you about what happened at the lab after we left."

He hesitated, looked at the door, then sat back down. As he started to talk, he would not meet her gaze.

"Not much, as it turned out," he said. "I'm sure you suspected that it was staged as much as I did. Dr. Drace and Nole did a lot of running about—outside to talk to the protestors; inside to tell us what was going on; back outside. Around and around."

"I doubt that they fooled anyone," she commented with a grin. Having finally looked at her again, he grinned back.

"Probably not. These people are almost comical in their

naivete. They really haven't a clue how to negotiate or how to manipulate people or discussions."

"When did everyone finally get to leave?"

"We left about an hour or so after you did. The rest of them stayed."

"Then you were attacked on the road."

"Yes, by another group of people, but I think they were associated with the ones outside the lab. It was a sniper attack, more or less. We hardly saw anyone, and I don't think there were more than two or three guns."

He continued with more details of what was said and done, answering her questions, elaborating here and there. As he talked, the attraction Iroshi felt for the younger man began to grow. There was an honesty in his words and in his manner that was very appealing. The directness of his gaze. The way he smiled once in a while. When she asked a question he did not care to answer, he said so. Little things, reminding her of Mitchell. Ensi would say that she always saw something of Mitchell in every man she was attracted to.

This was a short acquaintance, but they would have some time to get to know one another. These negotiations were quite likely to go on several more weeks, maybe months.

Suddenly, Logan looked at the clock on the opposite wall.

"Damn," he said softly. "I have to get back to our room." He stood. "I didn't realize I had talked so long. Lenora will be upset. I mean, Commissioner Cieras." His expression turned to one of frantic consideration, totally unlike his previous quiet assurance.

"I'll see you tomorrow," Iroshi said, saving him from searching for explanations or excuses.

"Yes. Of course." He grinned sheepishly. "Sleep well." He held out his hand.

"Thank you," she said, taking his hand. "Goodnight."

As before, he lingered over the handshake for several heartbeats. The warmth of his hand, the depths of his brown eyes, held her. At last, she released his hand and walked him to the door. As she turned to say goodnight once more, she found him standing close enough to feel his warmth along the length of her body. Impulsively, she reached up and kissed him lightly on the lips. His hand brushed her waist, sending shivers down her limbs. She smiled, drew away, and opened the door. He left without another word.

*Why do you always do this?* Ensi asked.

That was always the first line. Every time.

Iroshi resisted the temptation to ask, "Do what?" She knew perfectly well what he was talking about. What she didn't understand was why he always took on this air of disapproval.

The second night, after a long day of meetings that went nowhere, she and Logan had again met in her suite, talked a while, then gradually progressed to sex. A touch. A kiss. Then they dissolved into heavy breathing and a passionate embrace. The next night—last night—they talked afterward, just as wonderfully satisfying as the other way around. And as wonderful as any encounter she had experienced before. So many differences in men—their physiques, their techniques, rarely losing their ability to satisfy. She did love men.

However, this morning, Iroshi was paying the price and, although it was not unexpected, it did still irritate. Over the years, Ensi had never lost his opinion that her sexual escapades distracted her from the task at hand. She denied this vehemently, both to him and to herself. Success had always been theirs. Oh, there had been several years of quiet on the subject, after she met and gave up Yail. He had been a young policeman on Bosque at the time. Their short affair had seemed to threaten her relationship with Mitchell, and afterward she had been faithful. For almost seven years. But there was no denying her nature forever.

*You rarely do,* Ensi intruded.

"Oh, Ensi," she sighed. "I'm getting old. Don't try to deny me the few years of pleasure left to me."

The ensuing silence registered both regret and resignation. The two of them were so intertwined within her body and mind that they could read each other's feelings even without the possibility of body language and vocal inflection giving them away. It was difficult to remember the time when he was not there.

*All right, Iroshi. Take your pleasure with this man.*

"Remember how you insisted on calling me Laicy in the beginning?" she said, changing the subject only half deliberately.

There were times when the distant past was clearer than events of a week earlier. She shook her head. Although she had every reason to think she would live another thirty or forty years, there were times she was convinced she would not reach a hundred. There had been bad times when she had not wanted to get another day older.

She shook her head, shedding the route to self-induced depression.

*Yes, I remember,* Ensi said quietly. *There was good reason in those days. Or, we thought so.*

"What time is it?" she asked, suddenly afraid that she was going to be late for the morning meeting. She had risen earlier than usual and taken her time with getting dressed and eating breakfast.

*Only nine-thirty. We have plenty of time.*

She relaxed in the chair and sipped her tea. Eating breakfast alone was a habit she had developed several years earlier, even when Mitchell was alive. Some days, it was the only quiet time she had. That was why she resented it when Ensi announced they had visitors.

*The same two men we met on the road.*

"Now, what might they want?" she murmured.

When Jacob knocked on the door of the suite, she was tempted to tell him to send the men away. Her curiosity stopped her. The men who had been so secretive and threatening before were out in the open today. She called for Jacob to come in. He reported what she already knew.

"Have them come up," she said.

Getting to her feet, she pushed the button that retracted the table, dirty dishes and all. At the last moment she grabbed the teapot and her cup. No use wasting it.

Another knock on the door, and Jacob escorted the men into the sitting room. Erik followed them in. He and Jacob took places against the walls while Iroshi invited the visitors to sit. They took opposite ends of the same sofa, self-consciously looking over their shoulders at the two men standing behind them. The blond cleared his throat.

"We have something we would like to show you," he said without preamble.

*How deep do you want me to go?* Ensi asked.

She spread her hands wide, inviting the man to proceed.

"Are they the least bit sensitive?" she asked silently of Ensi.

*Not as far as I can tell.*

"I want to know exactly why they've come and what they want to show me."

"We couldn't bring it into the city with us," he said. He was the one who had been calmer during the encounter on the road. "We'll take you to it."

Jacob snorted a short laugh, and Iroshi allowed her frown to deepen.

"I don't know your names," she said icily. "I don't know what you are after or who you work for. You come without an appointment. I haven't the vaguest notion what you want to show me. And you want me to go with you!"

The dark-haired man jumped to his feet.

"You don't trust us but you want us to trust you?" he said loudly. "You'll turn us in, first chance you get."

He turned to glare a moment at his companion.

"First," she said in the same tone, "I don't give a damn about internal Djedian politics. Second, if I decide you need to be taught a lesson for any reason, I'll do it myself, or have one of my companions do it for me."

"Sit down, Dahrin," their spokesman said. He looked back at Iroshi, his expression guarded but resigned. "My name is Burgh Layton. My friend is Dahrin Pryhs."

*They have Prilly Jaxe,* Ensi cut in. *They found her before our meeting on the road. They think they know her secret but they are not sure. They are sure she or her condition, or both, have something to do with the persea.*

*No,* he said after a short pause. *They are the ones who sent her to you before. They have a contact at the hospital who knows who she really is.*

"Who is she?"

*As you surmised, she is Lisley Nole. The prime minister's wife.*

Four more days before landing on Djed. How in the hell was he going to stand it? Vieren touched his mind, tentative, pleading. Dukane lashed out with his own, punishing, hating. He felt her cringe, withdraw, weeping, if an animal could possibly weep. A touch of satisfaction almost made him smile.

Sandoval remained aloof, lying in his corner, always watching. He never reacted visibly or telepathically, but his hatred grew. A hatred that would make him very dangerous one day.

As Dukane watched, an extraordinary thing happened. At least, he found it extraordinary. Vieren got up from her corner of the cabin and moved to lie down next to Sandoval. Something she had not done in more than two years. A slight feeling of exultation crept to the edges of Dukane's mind.

"We'll have none of that," he said.

Vieren cringed at the image of punishment he projected but did not move away from her mate. Was her sense of devotion changing, or had Dukane misjudged it? Surely not. Too many years of subservience had passed, too much training and punishment.

He shrugged. Even so, this temporary mood would soon be remedied. Next to his bed hung a whip, a stick, and a small club. Primitive bits of persuasion, but they worked. He selected the stick, a small bit of wood with holes drilled through it so that it whistled in the air when he slashed downward with it. Vieren whined. Sandoval growled, low and quiet.

That would not do at all. They both needed a lesson.

# 10

❖❖

Snow fell outside in big puffy flakes, so thick that the house next door was hardly visible. Iroshi placed her right palm flat against the pane. Just as cold as before. Did the Djedians not use any of the modern insulating devices? The house had gotten downright chilly during the night, even for her, and she normally preferred cooler temperatures.

She shivered and looked at the clock for the fourth time. The visitors had left half an hour ago, and today's meeting with the Djedians and Athenians started in another half hour. She should be ready to leave, but she was not even dressed yet.

"Ensi, have Erik postpone the meeting."

*Until when?*

She considered that a moment.

"Can you find Nole from here?"

*I will see.*

The wind howled around the corner of the house, and the snowflakes began falling at a slight angle rather than straight down. She placed her hand against the pane again, then against her cheek. The coolness felt good now. She let the drape fall back into place. Living in this house made her feel very close to the elements, a feeling that she was not entirely comfortable with, now that the weather had turned bitter.

*I can reach him,* Ensi said.

"Tell Erik to reschedule the meeting for tomorrow. It's time we found out what happened to Nole's wife."

*Through Nole or Dr. Drace?*

She had already considered trying Dr. Drace—it was a reasonably sure thing that she would have been present at whatever incident had occurred. However, the emotional impact, the involvement, would be greater with Nole.

"Let's try Nole first. Any chance of Nole sensing you?"

*Just as well. I'm having difficulty locating Drace. Nole is not sensitive, plus he is busy at the moment.*

"Good. Find the memory and make sure he was there at the time."

She stretched out on the sofa and closed her eyes. No one would disturb her. Ensi had informed Erik what was happening at the same time he asked him to change the meeting time. She took several deep breaths. Relax. Distance. No emotion. Minutes passed. Much longer and she would drop into a meditative state. If that happened, she would feel everything Nole had felt at the time as if it happened to her; just as she had the first time Ensi had shown her an event from his past. She had been so unprepared.

Rousing slightly, she considered retrieving her tea, but it was stone cold by now.

*I am ready,* Ensi said softly. *This will not be easy.*

"They never are," she said and settled back down. "I'm ready."


Nole sits beside his wife's bed, holding her hand. Her breath comes as ragged whispers through parted lips. Her skin has become so translucent that the blood pulsing through her veins is almost visible.

He looks at the door, willing it to open. Drace promised to be back soon, but that was almost two hours ago. Time enough for doubts to have crept in. Persea has never been tested under these exact conditions, although there have been some decidedly nasty side effects under similar ones.

# PERSEA

Is Lisley strong enough to survive them? She doesn't even moan now, she has slipped so far away from him.

This would not be happening if his in-laws had only had their daughter inoculated at the correct age. But no. They were devout members of the temple, believing that the gods were the source of prevention and cure. Once she had passed the age of five, it was too late. Philella's fever, found only on Djed, was almost always fatal once contracted. The only prevention was inoculation before age five. Dammit! If those two fools were not already dead, he would kill them now.

He leans over and places his forehead against his arm on the bed. This latest crisis has lasted over twenty-four hours. Lisley holds on to life as long as he does the same to her hand. Twice he left for the bathroom and both times she nearly slipped away. He has to go again now, but is too afraid to leave her side.

The door swings open and Drace comes in. Nole jerks his head up, the movement shaking the bed slightly. Thankfully, Lisley is oblivious to it.

"Well?" He wants to shout but manages to keep his voice low.

Drace comes closer, a wide grin on her face.

"Everything looks all right," she says. "The blood tests don't reveal any problems. I discussed the situation with the other doctors and they believe, as I do, that we can save her."

"You didn't have much luck before."

"I know," she says, "but this should be different. Lisley is a much better candidate."

"But she's so weak."

"All the more reason to hurry before she gets weaker."

"Doctor," a voice calls from across the room. Nole jumps. He has forgotten the nurse was even there. "Mrs. Nole's blood pressure is dropping again."

"Damn," Drace says. "We must hurry."

She opens a green case, revealing several small vials containing a light pink liquid. Picking up an injector, she places one of the vials inside the chamber and closes it back up. She looks at Nole.

"One now, one in half an hour," she says.

Nole nods and grips his wife's hand a little harder. Drace moves to the other side of the bed. The nurse has already swabbed the upper arm. Drace places the injector nozzle against the arm and pulls the trigger. A soft sigh, almost human, and it's done. Nothing to do now but wait.

Quickly, Nole releases the hand and bolts for the bathroom. The added stress has made it impossible to wait any longer. Nothing seems to have changed when he returns. He sits, takes her hand in his, and tries to prepare to wait.

Ten minutes after the injection, Lisley's eyelids flutter slightly. Her breathing becomes more regular. She is going to make it! His prayers are being answered. Tears sting his eyes and he puts his head down on the bed again to hide them.

He would have sold his soul to the devil to save her. Instead, he sold it to an ambitious doctor whose promises may be coming true at last. All those people in the sanitarium helped make this moment possible, too. There was no way to thank them, of course, except by making the rest of their lives as comfortable as possible.

He senses movement and looks up. Drace approaches the bed with the injector in hand again. Half an hour has passed already? He must have dozed without realizing it.

"This should do it," she says.

The mechanical sigh sounds, and this time Lisley's arm jerks slightly. She felt it!

He looks at Drace again, and she smiles benignly. She moves to a chair on the other side of the room and sits down to wait.

# PERSEA 103

Nole lets out a sigh. He is so tired, but it will be worth it all when those emerald green eyes look into his once more. In spite of the tension, his own eyelids fight to close. He rubs both eyes with his fingertips, trying to smooth out the sand that seems to have gotten into them.

How long? Will she awaken tonight? Or will it be a day or two? He doesn't want to ask now, preferring to listen to the silence for any change.

Lisley grunts, coughs, lies still again. Her skin . . . Is it . . . Yes. It is pinker. He touches her upper arm. Warmer too. Could it be happening so quickly? Yes, please, let it happen now.

She twists her head on the pillow, side to side, gasps. Her hand suddenly grips his tightly. She is in pain! No. That is not supposed to happen. No pain.

"Doctor, her blood pressure has risen to two-thirteen over one-eighty-five. Her temperature is one-oh-five."

"It's just her body reacting to it," Drace says. "It will come down any time now."

"But such a high temperature . . ." Nole begins.

"It won't last long," Drace reassures him. "Only seconds. Believe me, it will be all right."

In another moment, Lisley's body convulses, the eyelids fly open, and she stares vacantly at the ceiling. Nole jumps to his feet, pulling her hand to his chest.

"Drace, what is happening?"

"Looks like we'll have to get her temp down after all. Nurse, cold packs!"

The slight body convulses again. The eyes move in their sockets, seeming to stare at Nole. The green is gone. That cannot be. They were always green. Now they appear black.

Lisley grits her teeth hard. Then her mouth opens in a silent scream. So much pain. No. It's not supposed to hurt!

Her back arches and she starts gagging.

"She's choking!" Nole yells.

Drace pushes between him and the bed. The nurse shoves several pieces of equipment up to the bed on the other side. Nole pushes the chair back and stands. Still feeling in the way, he rounds the chair and leans against the wall. He clasps his hands together, trying to keep them from shaking.

The frail body of his wife thrashes about while the two women try to work on her.

"Help us hold her down," Drace shouts.

No, he can't. He might hurt her, holding her so tightly. Get someone else. He walks to the door, opens it, and motions for two guards to come in. He points toward the bed.

"Do whatever Dr. Drace tells you to do," he orders, then resumes his place against the wall. The doctor gives him a withering look, then turns her attention to the newcomers.

"One of you at the foot of the bed, the other at the head," she tells them breathlessly. "Hold her down."

They move quickly, each grabbing hold of the woman they had so often saluted. By the looks on their faces, holding her is not an easy assignment.

Suddenly, Lisley's body stiffens. The two men let go, frightened looks on their faces. The doctor and the nurse pause in their efforts. The body relaxes and the eyelids slide open. The air becomes tainted with the smell of feces. He would not have believed there was anything left in that body to vacate in death.

"Send them away," Drace says, her voice strained.

Nole motions for the guards to leave. They do so hurriedly, keeping their eyes averted. If they are wise, tomorrow they will say they saw and heard nothing. Perhaps he should make sure. The nurse quietly leaves the room right behind the guards as they move into the hall.

Nole's knees are weak, and he cannot leave the wall for fear of collapsing. Drace presses Lisley's eyelids down, but they won't stay closed. She sighs and turns to the prime minister.

"Nole, I am sorry."

"You said . . ." he croaks. He clears his throat. "You said it would save her."

"I thought . . ."

"No more!" His voice is hard, and Drace looks frightened. "You will pay, Doctor. You will pay."

Gradually, the frightened expression leaves Drace's face. She straightens her shoulders and takes a step toward Nole.

"Don't forget, Prime Minister, that you had a hand in all this," she says bitterly. "There is abundant evidence of your involvement from the beginning."

His heart races, fear bringing his hands together again. If his part in all this comes out, he will lose his position as prime minister. He will lose the prestige he has built over so many years. There will be time later, an opportunity for vengeance. But not now.

He sighs and drops his gaze.

"I'm sorry," he says, putting as much contrition as he can into the words. "It's the strain, you see. Poor Lisley."

He closes his eyes and presses a tear from under each eyelid.

"I will miss her so."

How will he ever replace her? Who will stand by his side, support him, host the dinners, do all the things a leader's wife should do? Especially now that Djed is on the verge of gaining a more exalted place in the sector hierarchy.

No. First things first. Allay Drace's fears. Soothe her anger. He opens his eyes and finds her still watching him.

"We have to work . . ."

Lisley's hand quivers ever so slightly. He gasps. Drace turns to see what he is looking at. She sees it too. Immediately, she checks pulses—wrist, neck—checks the eyes.

She turns the monitor back on, checks for heartbeat and respiration. She looks back at him, her eyes full of hope.

"She's alive," she says triumphantly. "We've won."

It's impossible. He saw Lisley die. Yet her eyelids have just closed and opened again. The little finger on her left hand curls, bending the others slightly.

Elation sweeps through his body. She is coming back to him to take care of him again. Thank the gods. Even so, Drace will pay one day for her threat if nothing else. For the moment, he might still need her to keep Lisley on the road to recovery.

That road is short. Within days they discover, to their mutual dismay, that Lisley will never recover any further than the others who were also given the formula at the moment of death. She is moved to Pritchard Sanitarium, partly owned by Drace, and given the name Prilly Jaxe. Her resemblance to the prime minister's wife is often remarked on, but Mrs. Nole has reportedly gone south in hopes that the warmer climate will prove beneficial to her health. Speculation grows as to the true nature of the illness, since it has never been officially named. If it is Philella's fever, as has often been surmised, she would be dead soon, no matter where they moved her. Once the fever came on, no one recovered, and the end came within a few months. In his devotion to her, the prime minister would try anything, everyone knew that, but nothing would help. Nothing.

Nole makes contact with a group he knows about, one without much influence, but one that could help him. If he can manipulate them, and let the temple continue its campaign against persea, together they might bring the good doctor down, leaving him in complete control.

Iroshi opened her eyes. The window was in direct line of sight from where she lay on the sofa. Snow still fell as thickly as before. She looked at the clock. Two hours have elapsed. Gods, she felt as if she could hardly move. Might never move. Her eyes closed, and she listened to her own breathing.

A knock came on the door. "Come in," she said, but her voice was so low it could not have passed through to the hall. Still, the door opened. Soft light came on—one of the lamps, probably. Erik came to the sofa and knelt beside her.

"Are you all right?" he asked.

"Yes, I'm fine. Just tired, very tired."

He handed her a cup of tea and she sat up to take it. He had made it strong and sweet. Earl Grey. Very expensive and her favorite. With each sip, warmth flowed through her body, relaxed her. These sessions had always been exhausting, but it got worse as she got older. The day would come when they must be given up or take the chance that one would kill her.

Erik waited quietly out of sight. Snow fell outside. The warm glow from behind made the room a little lighter than the world under grey skies. Sleep would be wonderful. However, there were still things to do. Decisions to be made. Such as, what use could be made of this new knowledge? Erik was eager to know what she had found out. He would have taken the trip into Nole's mind if he could have, but he was not among those few of the Glaive who could travel the thread of others' memories. A lot of members wished they could. A foolish wish, given the exhaustion it always brought on.

She sipped the last of the tea. Cool. Had it cooled so quickly, or had she held the cup longer than she realized? Setting the cup on the nearby table, she called to Erik. Time to face it.

"Yes?" he answered.

He pulled a chair up to the sofa, and she began telling him what she had learned. His expression turned stoic, and anyone else might think the events had little effect on him.

After so many years, she knew him better. Deep disappointment etched lines across his forehead and around his eyes. He had never learned that although a people might be downtrodden, abused, or ignored, they were not necessarily worthy of assistance.

She finished, then relaxed and watched. A muscle twitched in his jaw, and for a long moment he stared at the floor. He lifted his head, their eyes met, and he smiled.

"What now?" he asked.

What indeed. This little effort to help a weak civilization deal with a stronger one was getting terribly complicated. Whatever the final outcome, the consequences would affect Djed in a big way, although the effect would be less for Athens. For the rest of humankind, what would be the consequences? They would be more those of omission than commission. At worst, people on far-flung worlds would not be offered the benefits of persea. Or would it be worse to have access to it? Was it time for the Glaive to begin making judgments on the advisability of actually producing persea?

She voiced these thoughts to Erik.

"On the one hand," she continued, "we have a group, led by the Patriarch. Their stated purpose is to quash this formula on moral grounds, while in reality, they want control. He told me about their export of the wine to let me know the temple is experienced in such things."

She handed him the mug and he ordered another. She lay back with her eyes closed until he brought the fresh one.

"On the other hand," she continued, after taking a sip, "we have a group, led by Nole of all people. They want to produce persea but keep control in the hands of the Djedians, leaving the Athenians and the Glaive out of the process totally. On the third hand, if we had one, are Drace, the scientists, the government, and the Athenians. They want to produce the formula, then work together marketing it."

Erik nodded agreement.

"Where in all this does the Glaive come in?" she went on. "On what side should we be?"

"In spite of Nole's defection, we began on the side of the government and the scientists," he said. "Is there any reason to change after all?"

The Glaive always strove to remain loyal to the side that originally hired it. That side was often selected or rejected based on its aims in the question. The senior members of the Glaive also considered which side offered the best advantages for the guild and its overall aims. If no prestige would attach to the Glaive, and the dispute had little overall significance, the request was sometimes rejected entirely, the Glaive taking no side at all. However, this time they had taken sides. It was the sides themselves that were changing the overall prospects.

"We certainly can't walk away from it now," Erik continued. "This is fast becoming a situation in which our image can end up more tarnished than enhanced."

"We could effectively destroy any trace of the formula: all knowledge, notes, people, even labs that contain any information at all."

Erik shook his head.

"Word would get out too easily. We have to go forward, bring the negotiations to some sort of finish and walk away. We have to at least appear to finish on the same side where we started."

*I agree,* Ensi said.

"That would mean destroying Nole," Iroshi reminded them. "If we do bring these negotiations to such a finish, we can't leave him here to try to work again to destroy Drace and all of her work. At the moment, she is more important than he is."

"Perhaps we could destroy them both," Erik said.

"We may have to."

# 11

❖

"She's gone!"

Pryhs stood in the doorway, scowling.

"What?" Layton cried. "You fool! How could you lose her?"

Pryhs stiffened, looked from his cohort to Iroshi.

"I didn't take her," Iroshi said in mock distress.

His scowl deepened. His hands balled into fists.

"Perhaps you should be asking who rather than how," she suggested to Layton. He turned back to his friend.

"Comb the area," he ordered. "Find her."

"We are and we will. You know how she wanders off," he added lamely.

Pryhs turned and disappeared into the darkness of the main part of the warehouse. Why did these people always hole up in warehouses? Iroshi glanced at her own companions in the small office. Jacob and Floyd stood at either end of the room, each close to one of the doors. Erik stood close to her elbow, at an angle to her stance so that he could keep an eye on both doors. In an instant he could be back to back or side by side with her in a defensive posture.

Layton walked over to the computer storage bank, placed an elbow on the top, and ran his fingers through his hair. His back was to her, but she could imagine the chagrin on his face.

*They are very embarrassed,* Ensi confirmed.

"They should be," she said. She turned to her companions. "I guess we might as well be going."

All three nodded and made ready to move to the door.

"Wait," Layton said, turning to face her at last. "She was here. And she is the prime minister's wife. I swear it."

"I believe you." She made as if to leave.

"But . . ." he began.

She stopped and looked him full in the face.

"What are you and your group trying to do here? Did you just want to embarrass the government? We've known for some time that Prilly Jaxe and Lisley Nole are one and the same."

He looked crestfallen at the news. Before he could respond, Iroshi went on.

"We also know that you are not the leader of this movement. You once were, but you gave way to someone else. Are you sure the new leader has the same goal that you do?"

"Of course he does!"

"You might want to be absolutely sure."

"After what happened to his wife, do you think . . ."

Realization spread across Layton's features. He had just fallen for a very old trick. How in the hell did these people hope to make it on their own? It was surprising that the temple had not moved in on them. The Patriarch and his followers were at least organized. Maybe even Roman could not tolerate this ineffectiveness. Yet they could, no doubt, be dangerous in their naivete.

"Look," he said. "All we want is to keep all management, production, and profits from persea in Djedian hands."

"Do you really believe Djed can produce and market it by itself? None of you has any of the necessary experience. Except possibly the temple."

Pryhs walked back in. From the look on his face, he had overheard the last statement and strongly disagreed.

"We can do anything we set our minds to," he said tightly. "We don't need anyone from the Glaive telling us what to do."

"Where is Prilly Jaxe?" she asked. His face turned crimson.

"We'll find her," he said. "Don't you worry."

She smiled derisively. "It doesn't matter to me one way or the other, but I doubt that you will." She glanced at Erik. "It's time for us to go."

"We can't allow that," Pryhs said.

He snapped his fingers and eight armed fighters stepped out of the shadows, behind and in front, blocking both exits. A couple of them held guns; the rest brandished swords, knives, and clubs.

"Don't be a fool," Layton said. He moved to block his partner.

"They know too much," Pryhs said. "They know where we are, who we are . . ."

"And who our leader is," Layton added. "If you try to keep these people here, we'll have more trouble than we know how to handle."

"They know about . . . about our chief? How could they?" Pryhs expression grew suspicious. "Did you tell them?"

"Yes. But, they already knew," Layton added hurriedly.

Layton looked over his shoulder at Iroshi, challenging her to deny it. He might be smarter than she had thought. If nothing else, he was the one who kept Pryhs from going off half-cocked, and that was not faint praise. One day, however, he would not be around at the right time.

He was now. He waved their people off. Pryhs's frown deepened. Although the others backed off at Layton's command, his jaws set tighter and his knuckles whitened where he gripped his own handgun. After a moment, his arms dropped. Without lowering his gaze from Layton's face, he moved toward the nearest door.

"We'll talk later," he said in a low, hard tone.

Still standing with his back to Iroshi, Layton sighed. Clearly, it was becoming more than he could cope with.

*He knows he is losing control of Pryhs,* Ensi said. *They are both frustrated by their lack of power and their failure, thus far, to accomplish anything. They actually hoped to bring the Glaive to their side.*

"That might not be a bad idea."

*Surely you do not want to keep the formula from being made available to everyone.*

"Oh, it will be available, and with the help of the Athenians. We must eliminate Pryhs somehow, though. He will be a constant source of trouble." Aloud, she said, "Layton, I know you want the best for Djed. So do we. Can we work together to find some kind of compromise?"

"Compromise?" Layton said distractedly. "What kind of compromise?"

"What do you hope persea will bring to your world? How do you see it being marketed?"

Layton rubbed his eyes with his fingertips in an effort to bring his focus back to the matter at hand.

"I thought you were set on the government's plan," he said. "The negotiations with Athens. All that."

"The Glaive was asked to make sure Djed made a good deal in negotiations with Athens. We still believe that is probably the best means of proceeding." Layton started to protest. "Hear me out," she said, cutting him off.

"The Athenians have a marketing network already in place, much more extensive than anything the temple has. They have numerous other contacts that could be of help in both producing and marketing persea. Join the talks. Let everyone hear your concerns. Listen to all the details of the current plan and the concerns from the other sides. Everyone wants this to work."

*Except Nole. And the church,* Ensi reminded her, but she ignored him.

Layton glanced out the door in the direction Pryhs had gone.

*He fears he is losing control. He fears that trusting you might be the most foolish thing he has ever done. He knows that many of his followers will consider it traitorous. Either path seems equally dangerous to him.*

"I hope he will see my offer as the best means of regaining that control."

"The Glaive can take no profit from this," she assured Layton. "We took on these negotiations pro bono—without compensation. We're on Djed's side. Our reputation could be irreparably harmed if we worked otherwise, and it's our reputation that keeps us in business."

He studied her a moment, then nodded. "All right," he said. "I'll listen."

"You're naturally worried about Pryhs and the others who believe as he does," she said. Layton nodded. "We will just have to convince them, won't we?"

"I don't believe that's possible," Layton said.

"We'll see. I can be very persuasive."

"I know."

She held out her hand. "Tomorrow. Ten A.M. The full negotiations are to resume at the Rohbins Conference Hall. We'll make arrangements to get you in."

He shook her hand and grinned. "Some of them won't like my being there."

"We'll convince them it's a good thing."

The large room was lit only by the fire in the massive fireplace. Some corners of the room flickered light and dark with the ebb and flow of the flames; other corners stayed ominously dark, particularly to a stranger.

Roman glanced over as Dukane stretched his legs toward the warmth, his chair pulled close, seeming to revel in the simple pleasure. Although the fireplace had been a conceit of sorts when first built, the Patriarch had come to appreciate its practicality as he grew older and his body grew colder. He wondered sometimes if that was what brought death to some—the body's cooling as the years piled on.

Although the thought danced through his mind, tonight his thoughts were more occupied with studying his visitor. In just over a day, Dukane had made himself felt by everyone within the temple's walls. For himself, the Patriarch felt fear that he could not explain even if he tried. The man spun its tendrils in his mind by his very presence. They must get this business finished as soon as they could and send him on his way.

Dukane reached down to scratch one of the animals he had brought behind the ears. She jumped in apprehension, and for a moment Roman thought he saw his own fear mirrored in her eyes. However, in an instant, she was purring, eyes closed as if enraptured by the attention.

He cleared his throat and Dukane looked over at him. Disdain turned down the corners of the stranger's mouth. How dare he show such disrespect to a man of his position? When this was all over, the former Glaiver must be taught some manners. For the time being, however, they needed his assistance.

"The fire feels good," Dukane said.

"I find it comforting on these cold nights."

"Hmmmm. But we must get down to business, mustn't we?"

Roman smiled and nodded. It was about time.

"I think we have found just what you need to destroy the formula and its creators," Dukane said.

"It is not our aim to destroy the formula. We simply want to make sure it is used properly."

"Of course," Dukane agreed, a smile playing about the corners of his mouth. "It is a gift of the gods, after all."

Damn his impudence! He would be taught not to mock the gods one day. Still, the phrasing was nice, the idea expressing the proper reasons for the temple becoming involved in this matter.

"You were gone a long time today," he said. "Did you get everything done?"

"Oh, yes. Would you like to see?"

"Of course."

"Then come to my suite and you shall."

Dukane got to his feet and started out of the room, followed closely by the animal. He walked rapidly and did not look back to make sure his host followed. Roman struggled to keep up, his breathing became labored, and his arthritic right knee shot pain through his whole leg. Even at that pace, Dukane looked at his surroundings as if he was planning on rearranging things, an attitude he had adopted since the first moment he had arrived.

This was definitely not the man they had expected to come to their aid, and it was clear they should keep a close eye on events, or they might lose control completely. If they hadn't already. This called for a meeting of the elders. Yes, right away.

Dukane stopped in front of his door, paused long enough to make sure the animal was at his side, then pressed the button. He stepped into the suite. Roman quickened his pace, afraid the door might be closed in his face. He swept into the room and stopped, struggling to catch his breath. As he did so, he swept the room with his gaze.

Cline, another of Dukane's companions, sat on the sofa where he had been polishing his sword. The weapon and the cloth had been set aside, and he was getting to his feet.

"Where is our visitor?" Dukane asked.

"In the small bedroom," Cline answered.

"This way, Your Holiness," Dukane said and, again, led the way.

Roman panted after, down the hall, second door on the right. Dukane stopped in front of it, rapped lightly with his knuckles, then opened the door. This time he stepped aside and let the Patriarch enter first.

Wessell, one of Dukane's followers, got to her feet and nodded to Dukane. Roman nodded to her as if acknowledging the greeting, but his eyes swept to the figure lying on the bed. She was so small, the bed so large, her size minimized by everything in her surroundings. How could a body so depleted of life continue to live? If it was actually alive.

"Is it really . . ."

"Lisley Nole?" Dukane finished. "Yes, it's she. Lovely, isn't she? Almost life-size. Almost alive."

He had been going to ask if it was alive, but Roman did not correct the interpretation of his question. It was partially answered anyway.

Dukane waved a hand at Wessell, who sat back down.

"She has to be watched," Dukane continued, referring to Lisley. "She tends to wander off a lot."

"Where did you find her? How did you know? Was it persea that did this to her?"

The questions tumbled out in rapid succession. In his excitement, he forgot his fear of the ex-Glaiver. Then Dukane spoke, his voice hardened by his sense of superiority.

"None of that was difficult, and it's not important," he said, dismissing the first two questions. "But, yes, it was the formula. They foolishly injected her at or near the very moment of death."

Roman could no longer still the question. "Is she truly alive or is she dead?"

Dukane walked to the bed and shrugged. "The body moves and functions, but there is nothing inside. Nothing." He reached down to touch the thin shoulder, his fingers moving to her arm.

Roman clapped his hands together. "I will order prayers for her soul," he said.

"There is no soul in that body. It left on schedule."

"Nevertheless, it is immortal and we will pray for her."

Dukane shrugged. "Do as you wish. However, we have more important things to consider."

Roman watched as his guest continued to caress the woman's arm. He shuddered slightly. Nothing about this man seemed to be natural.

"Not knowing much about your religion," Dukane said, "I cannot presume to plan how best to use Mrs. Nole's present existence. However, I would suggest you move quickly. I must remain totally in the background, of course."

"Of course."

Roman glanced at Wessell, but the woman seemed to be concentrating on an inner voice and paid little attention to their conversation. Lisley clearly had no interest in what was going on around her. He had never seen such blankness. It was as if she was an empty vessel waiting to be refilled.

"How long can she live like that?" he asked.

Dukane shrugged. "Maybe forever. I'm sure no one knows."

"If they did, they might not have given her the formula."

"You should be glad they did. It's your best advantage."

Roman nodded and released his grip where he had been holding his hands together too tightly. He stretched the fingers as if they were someone else's. Fear of the man gripped him again. So cold. So uncaring.

He left the apartment as soon as he could do so politely, returning to the great room and the fire. His body was

# PERSEA

colder than it had ever been, but still he was sweating. He removed the turban and wiped his bare head with a kerchief. The chair was warm against his back, and he extended his feet across the ottoman. As long as Dukane was in the temple, Roman did not think he would be warm again.

Dukane slumped on the sofa, his long legs stretched out in front of him. He had thought of going back into the great room to sit in front of the fire, but he wanted no interruptions or distractions. Still, the fire would warm him as nothing had been able to do since landing on this remote, two-bit world. His blood must have grown thin on Rune-Nelson.

Everything had gone well so far, and a smile played across his lips. Discovering Lisley Nole's existence and finding her in the old warehouse had been easy, since he was no longer bound by all the rules governing the reading of minds. Keeping his own presence on Djed a secret had proved to be as difficult as he had expected. Both Ensi and Garon made periodic sweeps to see who was within a certain distance of Iroshi, checking new arrivals and varying the times of their searches. It had helped that Roman and his people had maintained an old landing site some miles farther out from the city—something few knew about, it seemed. And, bringing nonmembers had helped too. They were more difficult for the companions to detect, especially since neither of the other companions knew his current staff members.

He had started to bring Glaive members, but he had realized that their assistance would have been made them more easily detected. Keeping up a barrier against detection was difficult at best, although it came naturally for him. He had been doing it all his life and he would bet that, aside from Iroshi herself, he was probably the very best at it.

Thinking of her suddenly brought memories of their last encounter. She had been magnificent, both defending and attacking. The sword a real extension of her own body and mind. Still the consummate warrior. Another reason to end it all now, before further decline set in. If she could only accept his knowledge, his anticipation of what the future held.

A sexual joining between him and her would be the ultimate accomplishment, of course. Mating with a goddess would raise him to godhood. Then the number of followers would grow among members of the Glaive. Worshipping the two of them would become a requirement for membership. Of course, all of the original companions would have to be purged.

Of course! Persea. As the older hosts lay dying, inject them with the formula so that the bodies became like that of Lisley Nole, trapping the companions inside. Or would they be? There must be a way.

Damn! Taking over the Glaive might not be as difficult as it had seemed, although such a scheme would take a number of years to complete. Once Iroshi was dead, there would be little to stop him. She must die suddenly, without warning, so there would be no time to go into revay, for her or Ensi. That much could be arranged, was being arranged. So could ensuring that there would be no body to find. That would add to the mystery.

Too bad it all had to happen on Djed, a world in the middle of nothing.

# 12

✦

Logan Rhiel stood in the hall outside the conference room. Cieras had just left him to go inside. She had moved stiffly, and from what Iroshi knew of the Athenian, that indicated anger. Iroshi dismissed the negotiator from her mind as she and her constant guards approached Logan. He and his boss had moved back into their own quarters early the night before, but he had paid a late visit. The memory of their time together was still fresh enough to be exciting. And a little scary.

She was not sure yet, but he was sounding and acting like he was falling in love with her. In the beginning, he had been fascinated with who she was: Iroshi of the Glaive, considered by some to be the most powerful woman in the empire. Then, his lovemaking had been tentative, as if he was not quite sure he had the right to be there. With each meeting, he had become bolder, more sure of himself. Last night, he had touched her mind with his. Not deliberately, but in his ecstasy, his own defenses had weakened and passion had burst through, a unique experience for both of them.

Logan caught sight of her, smiled, and started toward her. That smile made her heart skip a beat. It was so easy to fall in love with someone who was already in love with her. Was she assuming too much? Had it only been passion after all and not love she had felt from him?

As he drew closer, he held out a hand. Another surprise.

They had been careful not to give any hint of the relationship growing between them because of Cieras's fondness for him and her influence over his career. Not to mention Drace, who had some feelings for him too. Iroshi took his hand, and his smile widened, while a slight shiver ran through her at his touch.

*This is silly,* she thought, but only for a moment. It just felt too good.

He turned to walk beside her toward the door of the conference room. Jacob and Floyd kept a discreet distance.

"What's going on?" she asked.

His smile faded slightly. "I told Cieras about you and me this morning."

She stopped and faced him. "Was that wise? My god, Logan. Your career."

He shrugged but met her gaze without flinching. "I gave it serious thought last night after I got back to my room. I can't continue working with her. Her temper tantrums. Her possessiveness." She started to interrupt, but he cut her off. "I decided to get into the Glaive if you'll have me. If not, I can find work in many different places. My experience is a very saleable commodity."

"Yes, but . . ."

"It's done, Iroshi," he said. "I'm no longer part of the Athenian delegation, of course. And it probably would not be good form for me to work with the Glaive just yet." He smiled again.

"We had better get inside," he continued. "The meeting is supposed to start soon." He turned to move toward the door but stopped. "I don't mean to cut you off. I would like you to think about my joining the Glaive, if you will. Not because we're lovers, but because I'm well qualified." He went silent as one of Nole's people walked around them and into the conference room. "This isn't a rash decision. Finding a new position is something I have considered for a long time before we even met."

She sighed. "We'll talk about it later," she said. "I suppose you'll be needing a place to stay now." He nodded. "I'll have your things moved into our house. Meantime, we had best go in." He frowned, and she put her hand on his arm. "I'm not upset about your decision. At the moment, there are too many things going on to give it the attention I would like to."

He nodded his understanding, but the smile did not return to his lips. Had he expected her to be elated by his revelation? If so, his timing was off.

*Everything he said is true,* Ensi reported. *His considering the possibility of working in the Glaive is sincere and his desire to leave the Athenian service is long-standing.*

"All right," she said silently. "We'll talk with him tonight. Is Layton here?"

*Waiting in the anteroom as you ordered. No one knows he is there.*

"Good."

Inside now, she took her assigned seat at the round table. Logan took a chair against the wall behind her. A few gazes with raised eyebrows were sent in his direction, but no one seemed curious enough to approach him, although they had to realize something had happened.

"I don't have as good a feeling about this as I did," she said to Ensi.

*There is a lot of tension in here this morning. Cieras is very upset about Logan. Ah, and Nole. His wife going missing has him very worried.*

"He should be."

Nole stood and cleared his throat. "It looks like we are assembled now," he began. "We can get started . . ."

Iroshi stood. "Not quite, Mr. Nole," she said. "I have invited a representative of another interested party to join us. I think he may have some valuable input into these negotiations."

Ensi signaled Erik in the anteroom, and he nodded to Layton. Other than her own people, no one knew whom she was speaking of. Not even Logan.

"Mr. Burgh Layton and his people have a strong interest in this issue," she continued. "He has agreed to attend in an effort to prevent any future confrontations."

The two men entered through a door opposite her and moved slightly to her right and behind. Reaction rippled around the room. Most expressions reflected surprise. Others—Nole's and Cieras's in particular—showed anger.

"I won't have it," Nole exclaimed.

Cieras slowly got to her feet. "This is an insult," she said coldly.

Everyone else started talking or shouting at once, few supporting Layton's presence.

Iroshi glanced at Logan. He grinned and shook his head.

Pryhs strode down the street, followed by his usual entourage of eight supporters, all dressed in civilian clothes, but carrying swords at their sides. They looked as grim as he felt.

Layton had disappeared the day before, just walked out without a word. It was that damned Glaive woman. She had lured Layton away from the warehouse and, worse, from the cause.

The negotiations would be resuming soon; that was where Layton would be. It was time to do one of two things: rescue him from himself, or eliminate him and bring their leadership down to one. Two, if you counted Nole. However, Iroshi had been right about one thing. Nole's agenda was not the same as theirs.

He glanced over his shoulder. The nine of them should be able to handle whatever guards were at Rohbins Conference

Hall. There probably would not be many, since they knew of no reason to be afraid.

Pryhs quickened his pace, eager to have the whole thing resolved. His right hand rested on the butt of the laser pistol hidden under his jacket in his side holster. In spite of his best efforts, it was the only gun available on such short notice, the rest of their guns being out at different sites for training. It would be enough. Six of his companions were the best sword wielders in the movement, which boasted well-trained, well-practiced warriors. He had seen to that himself, while Layton kept trying politics and diplomacy. Most of the warriors were loyal to Pryhs, and this group in particular followed him without question. He had given them special attention from the beginning when he saw how good they were. He would put them up against the best on any world.

He raised his hand and slowed their pace as they neared the last corner. He moved to the building and stood with his back to it. The others lined up behind him, waiting silently as he edged around the corner and looked toward their target. This part of town was fairly isolated, and the street was empty. Two men stood guard, one on either side of the double doors of Rohbins Conference Hall. They could be handled easily, but that might take away the element of surprise. Yet he had no patience for going around to check the back. And the street remained empty, so they just might get inside without much fuss.

He motioned Lavillah to come up beside him. She was very good with her hands.

"Two guards at the door, Lav. You and I are going to get rid of them."

She nodded.

"We'll walk up to them, just like we planned," he continued. "They aren't expecting any trouble."

He waved to the others to wait and then moved around

the corner with Lavillah coming up beside him. Casually, they approached the building and climbed the broad stairway. The guards came to attention, studying the strangers.

"Hold there," the one on the right called out. "This building is restricted."

"We have a pass," Pryhs said, and reached toward his pocket.

He continued up the steps, getting closer to the guard, who reached toward his own gun. Lav hung back a little, keeping an eye on the second guard. The first one looked toward his companion. Pryhs hit him with a heart punch. The second guard had his gun free as he stepped across. The first crumpled. Lav took the two remaining steps at one time and caught him in the side with her foot. He grunted and fell sideways away from her. Pryhs turned and moved toward him. Lav closed in and put him down with a knee to the side of his head.

Neither guard moved. The rest of his team ran up, gathering in front of the doors. Pryhs drew his pistol and signaled for them to wait again, and he and Lav stepped gingerly inside. The lobby was empty. Element of surprise intact. Didn't these people believe in security? He nodded to Lav, who opened the door and called the others inside. They carried the two unconscious guards with them, placing them on the floor to one side of the foyer.

Pryhs studied the three closed doors within view. According to the floor plans they had studied back in the warehouse, the largest conference room was the center one. That was where they would all be and where a great deal of noise was coming from. He nodded toward the center door. Garvin and Fryeh moved ahead and flanked the door, their swords drawn. He put one hand on the door handle and pressed his ear against the door. A hell of a lot of shouting on the other side. He pulled back and nodded to Lav.

Pressing the latch button, he jerked the door open. Lav

rushed through the door, then to the left. Pryhs charged into the room and raised the pistol, firing a shot at the ceiling. Behind him, the other seven rushed in with swords drawn and began encircling the back of the room. Lav pushed three men away from the wall toward the table. Voices quieted, faces showed surprise, some still showed anger.

Layton stood near the round table, flanked by the two Glaivers. All three had turned to face him at the sound of the shots.

"You see," Nole shouted from across the room. "You bring that man in here and look what happens."

"Shut up," Pryhs ordered, pointing the gun at the prime minister. He turned back to his partner. "Layton, you're coming with us."

"Pryhs, don't . . ." Layton began.

"You come with us, or you die right here."

"Don't be a fool, Pryhs," Iroshi said. "Layton is here of his own accord, trying to iron out the differences between your people and the government."

"Not this way," he said. She took a step toward him. "Stop right there," he said. "You may have a reputation as a warrior, but that doesn't count for much here. And I don't think even the great Iroshi could outrun an energy beam."

"Layton, do you want to return with them?" she asked, never taking her eyes off the intruder.

"No," he answered. "We can work this problem out without violence."

"Damn you!" Pryhs shouted.

Iroshi spun to her left, pulling the sword free in the quick draw she had learned so long ago. The beam hit the chair she had been standing in front of. Acrid smoke rose into the air where the plastiwood was burnt. The pistol swung toward her. It fired. She swung the blade, deflecting the beam. The sword vibrated and she barely hung on.

Crying out in her distinctive kiai, Iroshi rushed Pryhs, knocking the gun from his hand. He just had time to draw his own sword. He was terribly off guard now, and she pressed her advantage.

The red haze descended through her as their swords met. With the second swing, the void came over her. She knew his surprise at the strength of her attack. She knew Floyd fought the woman. She knew Jacob and Erik fought others of the intruders while most of the delegates rushed out of harm's way. A couple of guards rushed into the conference room from a door at the back, but they had a difficult time defending against the better trained rebels.

All of this became part of her being as she became one with her surroundings. The void reached out, encompassing it all.

"Layton must not attack his own people," some part of her mind said.

*I will see to it,* Ensi answered.

At Ensi's internal command, Erik backed away from his adversary, placing himself between Layton and any attack. Meanwhile Pryhs, overcoming his surprise, began showing true swordsmanship. He had been well taught, better than the official guards she had seen. A shame to lose such talent.

His relative youth balanced her superior skill, and she found herself using every bit of that skill. Although his movements seemed slowed, her own just were not as fast as they once were. The question was, how long would her strength hold out? The last test had been a very brief one.

*Behind you,* Ensi shouted.

She sidestepped, just avoiding another blade aimed at her from behind, the move taking her out of Pryhs's reach. Quickly, she pushed the new blade downward in its original course, pressing it against the stone floor. Twisting the katana, she thrust backward, catching the man in his left hip, piercing upward through his abdomen. His scream was distorted. The man fell back onto the floor, pulling her sword free. She spun around as Pryhs sliced horizontally, catching her tunic. Her blade was high. She continued her spin, arcing the blade over his head. His forward momentum brought him closer. He was just recovering from his own swing when hers caught him in the right shoulder.

Pryhs managed to pull back and keep hold of his sword. However, he was bleeding badly.

Something touched her mind. It had been there for some time but the excitement of the fight had veiled it from her consciousness. She shrugged it away mentally, concentrating on Pryhs.

"Give it up," she panted.

"No!"

He rushed forward with sword upraised, supported almost solely in his left hand. She caught the blade with her own as it swung downward and pushed him back. With another kiai, she stepped in and caught him in the abdomen with a horizontal cut. Pryhs stopped, swayed, and dropped to his knees.

"I thought you were a myth," he said through the pain.

The void faded, the red haze fell away. She stood panting, watching him as he sat back on his heels. One hand was pressed against the wound in his abdomen, while the other still held onto the handle of his sword.

"It was supposed to be easy," he said, and fell facedown onto the stone floor.

Seeing that their leader had fallen, the three remaining intruders shouted their surrender and dropped their weapons to the floor. Iroshi continued to look at Pryhs, sadness touching her mind a moment. No use in that now, though. The man had knowingly placed himself at risk, and there was little sympathy to spare him for his foolishness.

She looked around the room and realized that Layton was gone.

"Where . . ."

*Logan took him into the anteroom.*

"Well," she said silently. "Logan may not be a warrior, but he knows when to act."

Nole started shouting for the guards to take charge of the prisoners, and Floyd and Jacob relinquished them at her signal. The two came to stand near her once again, as did Erik.

"Everyone all right?" Iroshi asked them.

"Yes."

"No problems."

"Not a scratch."

"Let's get Layton back in here," she said.

*He is on his way,* Ensi informed her.

"How?"

*Logan. He is receptive, you remember.*

"Yes, but . . ."

*He took Logan back when I asked him to. Everyone else was too busy and I knew you did not want Layton to have to fight his own people.*

"Right."

The two men entered the conference room, and Layton headed straight for Iroshi. Logan followed close behind, his brow tight with tension.

"What the hell do you think you're doing?" Layton growled. "Those were my people."

"They would have killed you if you had decided not to go with them."

"They wouldn't have. Pryhs and I worked together for years."

"Layton," she said softly. She looked around to make sure no one else could hear. "He intended to kill you if you did not come to your senses as he thought you should. He hated these diplomatic machinations and wanted to bring your group back to your original, active policies."

"Maybe he was right."

"No, he was not right. All your group could ever accomplish was to be a nuisance at best, a spoiler at worst. However, you would never be able to keep persea from being disseminated among the worlds of the empire. That is inevitable. Too many people know about it already."

"If I go back . . ."

"If you go back, they may treat you as a traitor. No one really knows what your role was in all of this, except the few of us. I'm afraid you're stuck with us from now on. We can make sure your true role is known, or we can encourage your people to think the worst. If you choose to abandon us, they will have to be destroyed in order for this business to proceed. If they become convinced you really were working for the good of everyone, you might become a hero."

"I never wanted to be a hero," Layton said slowly.

"Too late now."

She looked around the room again. The prisoners had been taken away, and calm was beginning to descend. Nole glanced toward Layton several times as he discussed events or plans with his staff. Nole could never be sure who his erstwhile partner might have told about his own involvement with the guerrillas. They would distrust each other from now on.

Layton saw her looking in that direction and spared a glance at Nole.

"How are you going to convince him?"

She shrugged.

"He won't say anything. His own head is on the block right now. Just don't turn your back on him."

"Ladies and gentlemen," Nole called. "Can we please resume our seats?"

"Make sure you have a bodyguard around," Iroshi added as she and Layton took their seats. There was a general rustling as everyone complied with Nole's request. "There must be some people in your organization you can trust."

Layton nodded.

"I gather the consensus is that we should continue with the meeting," the prime minister continued.

Everyone nodded agreement.

Cieras rose, and Nole recognized her.

"I wish to protest this entire affair," she said. "It would seem that Iroshi and her Glaive have placed all of us in jeopardy with this unilateral action they have taken."

Iroshi tented her fingertips and sat back in her chair, resisting the urge to smile. Things were going to get much more interesting.

She felt Logan's presence very strongly behind her, and she turned to glance at him. His expression was troubled, and in a flash she understood that he knew more than she had wanted him to know.

The car moved slowly along snow-lined streets, its progress throwing up dirty water from snow melted on the heated road surface. The coldness of the scene outside the windows lessened the effect of the heater, and Iroshi shivered. A slight reaction to the events of the day, too, although everything had gone very well.

Logan, sitting beside her, was clearly struggling with his own reaction to those same events, and blaming her for setting them into motion. Although he struggled against the urge to read actual thoughts, his sensitivity was so strong that he often caught emotions and intentions on the surface enough to know what went on in someone's mind. Particularly when their thoughts were very strong.

As hers had been during the fight. Once Logan had taken Layton to safety, Ensi had been preoccupied with watching her back. Neither of them had realized how tied into their thoughts the Athenian had become.

*You cannot invite him into the Glaive just on that basis,* Ensi said suddenly.

There was a time when such an intrusion would have startled her and, possibly, made her angry. However, after so many years, his words were expected.

"It seems as good a reason as any," she countered.

*We have not done a full scan as yet. There are too many things we do not know about him.*

"We thought we knew everything about Dukane, and look what happened."

*He had stronger talents than we imagined. Just because we made that mistake, we do not have to make another.*

"Speaking of Dukane," she said, and paused. She hesitated to mention the feeling she had experienced twice during the day, preferring to attribute it to the strain and excitement. However . . . "Did you sense a presence just when everything went to hell in the conference room this morning?"

*What presence?*

"I could have sworn I felt Dukane's presence. Just for a moment. Then, later, something else."

*Something else? What sort of something?*

Iroshi shivered slightly and Logan, feeling it where their arms touched, glanced over at her. Without hesitation, he put an arm around her shoulders and pulled her close. She smiled and leaned against him, knowing better than to accept his gesture as full forgiveness. On the other side, Erik glanced at them out of the corner of his eye. He and Garon were eavesdropping on the internal conversation.

"It's been a very long time," she said to Ensi. "It was such a brief moment today. But . . . it felt like a booreecky."

Ensi shivered too, and did not answer for several minutes, a sign that he was reviewing his own memories.

*Dukane has been so strong in our minds since we arrived here on Djed that I thought it was just a shadow of memory,* he said at last. *I also felt both incidents. Strange that there was no hint of Paige.*

"Do you still believe it's just a memory then?"

*It does not seem logical that he would have followed us here.*

"But he still has not been found."

*I know.* They fell silent. The car turned onto their street. *Perhaps we should send for a few more members,* Ensi suggested at last. *Just to be safe.*

"If he can block us from detecting him, what good would that do? Besides, we have the racer crew if we need reinforcements."

*If he plans on doing anything, he will have to let his guard down eventually. With enough people, we can monitor more closely.*

That much made sense, of course. As far as she remembered, though, there were no members within easy distance.

"No, with everything that's happened, we're close enough to closing this deal that I don't think there's time to arrange all that. Another couple of weeks ought to do it. Besides, everyone is occupied with their own assignments."

The car pulled into its assigned parking place in front of the house. Jacob cut the engine, opened the door, and stepped out.

"Call one or two if—and only if—they are in a position to leave without jeopardizing their work."

Jacob opened the back door, and Iroshi stepped into the cold. She moved away from the car but stopped to listen. The sounds of the world were muffled by the snow, making it feel as though everything was close around her. This kind of closed-in feeling had never been claustrophobic.

She stuck out her tongue and caught several large snowflakes. One caught in her eyelashes, and she laughed. All four men looked at her and grinned. With difficulty she resisted the urge to make a snowball and throw it at one of them.

# 13

❖

Dukane strode through the temple lobby, heading for his own rooms. He felt like dancing his way there, but the templars would be scandalized by such behavior within the walls of their place of worship. And to think that his wonderful mood was all their fault. Well, not all, but in large part.

Their minds were full of events outside the building. Everyone's minds were full of the same events; however, he could not scan those outside as safely as he could those inside. Thank goodness he had these minds to search. Otherwise he would be longer in finding the final outcome that they condemned so heartily. Oh, the indignation, the amazement. They condemned Iroshi for setting in motion the events that led to this Pryhs's death. All the while, he applauded her. Such a bold step.

In one afternoon, she had eliminated Pryhs and his followers: an obstacle; bonded a faction to her own side: Layton and those loyal to him; and placed the prime minister in a most precarious position. Poor man. He was besieged from all sides now. No more than he deserved, of course. He was totally out of his league.

Once in his sitting room, Dukane paced for a time. Such a stroke! Further reason to admire Iroshi. Further proof that the time was at hand for ending it: she was at the height of her career. Even she would not want to wait until she was in decline. Everyone would remember her this way.

He sat in a chair, but could not sit still. Paige was being sullen, as she had been almost since their first moment on Djed. Back on his feet, he resumed pacing and remembering. In his excitement, he had nearly made a fatal mistake. He had gotten too close. Iroshi had nearly felt his presence. Ensi had been too busy watching on all sides for any threat. He frowned, both in relief and frustration. If she had taken the time to enhance her sensitivity, as he had done years ago, she would not have missed him.

He shook his head and sat back down. It could have been an irretrievable error had he been detected. He should have resisted the temptation, but being with her as she fought, even for only a moment, was something not to be missed whenever the opportunity arose. Few in the Glaive had ever experienced it. The only thing better would be to . . .

Best to leave that thought unfinished. Still, images crept into his mind, fantasies of how it might have been. He jumped to his feet and made his way to the back bedroom. He opened the door softly and went in. Wessell sat in her chair, eyes closed, meditating. She would never accept that she had no extraordinary mental powers, and was always trying to conjure them out of thin air.

Dukane took a sniff of the air and frowned. Damn the woman. She had sat there and let Mrs. Nole soil herself again. He stepped up to his follower and kicked her in the shin. She cried out. Her eyes flew open. She reached for the pained limb. He grabbed her by the hair and pulled her to her feet. Holding her in a crouch, he pulled her toward the bed.

"Can you smell that?" he shouted at her.

"Yes," Wessell whimpered.

"If you cannot do the job you are here to do, I will send you back to the ship."

"No, please, Dukane. I'll do better. I promise."

"You damn well better, you incompetent whore." He released her hair with a shove. "Now, get her cleaned up and this room aired out."

She sprawled on the floor next to the bed. "Yes, Dukane."

She cowered there, eyes downcast. He resisted the urge to kick her again, knowing that fear rendered her unable to move already. She would not obey until he had left the room and her nerves had calmed. To speed things up he could say soothing words, caress her, and she would almost purr, like the booreecki.

Instead, he dismissed her with a sneer and a wave of his hand. The bitch had spoiled his good mood, and he badly needed to recover it. He had to find Vieren. The adoring animal often had a soothing effect at times like this. He went in search of the female booreecky but changed course before finding her.

The taste of Iroshi earlier had reawakened the longing that never fully went away. A longing that he must fulfill before it was no longer possible to do so. She had the new lover; they made love every night, as far as he had been able to determine. There would be no trouble finding her. Just once. He might never have her physically, but he could have her psychically. Even more intimate than any other man would ever know.

Tonight, then. No need in waiting. Even if she detected his presence—which he doubted—it would be worth the risk. It might put her on guard, of course, but that would not help anyone. Not her. Not Nole or Cieras or Layton. None of them would escape him. Oh, her passing would be well attended. Many souls would accompany her to whatever heaven or hell awaited her. Her passing would be magnificent.

He glanced at his watch. Not yet mid-afternoon. He must find something to pass the rest of the day. Ten o'clock would be the right time to seek her out.

The rest of the afternoon he spent restlessly pacing from room to room, alternately petting and cursing vieven, and checking his watch. In early evening he returned to the back bedroom. Wessell had cleaned up their guest and her bed, and there had been no more accidents. She leapt to her feet when he entered. He sniffed deeply—some sort of flowers scented the air. He nodded approval, and she beamed.

He moved to the bed and looked down at Mrs. Nole. He reached out with his mind. Nothing. There was nothing in that head. No thought, no fear, no memory. Being inside her was very like strolling through an empty building with halls and rooms where footsteps echoed back at you. If he shouted, he was positive he would hear his own voice bounce back.

He closed off, turned on his heel, and left the room. Something about that emptiness drew him deeper inside, and he feared he would never find his way out if he stayed too long. Paige refused to even try it for a moment. Wessell stood in the same place as he closed the door, waiting and hoping for some sort of recognition.

Three more hours before he could seek Iroshi out. He strolled outside his apartment, trying to occupy himself. The temple was fun, a distraction. He could imagine, as he moved from one room to another, how the whole complex would look if it were the seat of his new religion. His wandering made Roman nervous, which was part of the fun. Did that stupid old man think that such a deity as Iroshi could be enthroned on a third-rate world like Djed?

Of course, since Iroshi would die here, this world's importance would be greatly enlarged. It would become a place of pilgrimage. He could imagine members of the Glaive roaming these halls and chambers, in full uniform, welcoming the uninitiated. The Glaive would become so powerful, no one could gainsay anything its new leader wanted. Of course, the most logical choice as leader would be himself, the architect of the new organization. Oh, gods, it would be glorious! If he survived. If he did not, his followers would see that he was enthroned beside her.

Dukane rounded a corner in the hallway and almost stopped short. Straight ahead, two priests stood before a door at the very end, clearly guarding it against intruders. He realized that he had been drawn this way subconsciously, and he searched beyond them. Who was there? What was so important? He set Paige to identifying those within and turned his attention in another direction, finding Vieren and Sandoval.

"Come to me," he called.

His immediate hesitation was slight, but he slowed his pace further, realizing that he had entered a part of the temple in which he had never been before. That would probably mean that the room at the end of the hall was the council chambers.

*Yes,* Paige confirmed. *The Patriarch is there, and most of the councilors. Only thirteen of the fifteen.*

Ah, this was not a regular meeting, but one called for a special reason. His presence, of course. Did they plot to get rid of him already? Not so easily done.

As he neared the guards, Dukane made eye contact with both, first on the right, then on the left. That made them uneasy enough. With no effort, he and Paige froze them where they were, rendering them unable to move. In the distance the two booreecki responded to his summons. He thumbed the control to the right of the door, and it opened inward. He strode into the room, stopped just short of the table, and stood with both hands on hips.

Roman's head jerked up to look at the intruder, a scowl on his face. That look instantly turned to recognition, then surprise. Farlow, seated on the Patriarch's right hand, started to rise, then thought better of it. The councilors, seated along each side of the table, looked first at Dukane, then, one by one, at Roman. If they expected guidance from His Holiness, they soon realized they were mistaken as he sat speechless, face blanched with fear.

Dukane turned, grabbed a chair from along the wall next to the door, and set it at the end of the table opposite Roman. The two booreecki had entered the room and now took positions right behind him as their master sat in the chair. They sat on their haunches, each watching the robed figures.

"Sorry for barging in like this," Dukane said into the total silence that had descended. "I feel sure that you've been meaning to invite me to one of your meetings and just overlooked it."

*They've been discussing how to get rid of you,* Paige reported. *Their fear of you is almost palpable. Farlow, in particular, has spoken out against you.*

"I know," Dukane responded silently. "Our two pets feel their fear strongly."

With the hair standing up on their backs, Sandoval and Vieren nearly drooled in their excitement. They felt the fear in the room as animals can when confronted with helpless creatures.

"Please continue," Dukane said aloud as he leaned back in the chair. "I'm just here to listen."

"We had just finished," Roman said.

He looked around at his underlings, who all nodded. He stood in dismissal. The priests looked down as they followed suit. In ones and twos they got to their feet and left the room, led by Farlow. Roman held Dukane's gaze as his people filed out, some of them muttering uneasily to companions, others moving silently. None would look at Dukane or the booreecki as they passed. The old man was showing some spunk after all, rather like a rat trapped in a corner. The man's courage would not last, however, for he was too easily cowed.

"Sit!" Dukane commanded.

Roman dropped into his chair, a look of terror now spreading across his features. Dukane laughed aloud at the Patriarch's fear. Being controlled from within was an entirely new type of threat—one he was not prepared to consider, much less confront.

Then, the beginnings of understanding.

*He has never experienced mental control,* Paige said. *He's accepted that it could exist, though. Now he's making the logical connection to the Glaive. He's thinking of Iroshi.*

"Feed him the idea that all such power comes from her," Dukane said. "See what he does with that."

He stood and walked between his two pets, toward the door. Two of the priests standing just down the hall opened their mouths to protest, but their words were cut off. The guards, although released from their paralysis, did not move a muscle.

He closed the door and returned to his chair, while Roman sat watching his so-called guest, unaware that many of the thoughts racing through his head were not his own. Every few seconds Paige checked to see if anyone was picking up her activity from outside the temple. She flashed a minute all-clear to Dukane each time. In a matter of two more minutes, it was done, and Dukane moved to a chair nearer the Patriarch.

"Now we can talk," he said expansively.

He released his hold on the old man, who slumped noticeably. The look and feel of fear remained as he waited for Dukane to speak.

"I've decided there will be no further meetings," he said at last. "They aren't necessary at the moment."

"Who are you to make such decisions?"

"Why, I'm your guest and you must humor me. Besides, the most important thing right now is to gain control of the formula, isn't it? We should be concentrating all our efforts in that area."

He stood, stepped around the chair, and placed his hands on the back.

"I assume that we understand each other," he said.

Roman continued to stare at the tabletop, not wanting to answer. But, as the silence dragged on, he accepted that he had no choice.

"Yes, we understand each other."

"Good."

Dukane left the room without another word, the booreecki trotting close behind. The guards had finally abandoned their post, and no one stood about the hall. His footsteps and the click of the animals' claws on the stone floor echoed off the walls.

*Farlow and five others are waiting on the other side of the main sanctuary,* Paige reported.

"Yes. What do they plan on doing?"

*Three with knives for you and three with a net for Sandoval and Vieren.*

Dukane looked down at the two. Their hackles were raised. They, too, sense the trap awaiting them. They almost skipped in their excitement. It had been a very long time since they had been allowed to hunt.

*Can we avoid this fight?*

Dukane snorted.

"There's no other way back to our suite," he said. "Are you losing your nerve?"

*Of course not.*

"Are the templars?"

*Losing their nerve? They're frightened. I don't think they had a nerve to lose among them.*

"We'll teach them to trust their instincts, won't we?"

The booreecki's heads went down in their hunting stance. The three of them moved through the sanctuary, not trying to move quietly. No use in letting the six darling priests know their element of surprise was long gone.

Just shy of the ambush, Dukane instructed his pets to project. Give those waiting a taste of primitive, alien mental processes. Let them know what was planned for them.

Even as far away as he was, he heard at least one gasp. Few humans could experience those images without disgust and fear. Vieren and Sandoval had come to enjoy the taste of human flesh—something he had included in their special diet to encourage their appetite for it.

Quietly, Dukane drew his sword from the sheath across his back. The Great Pallasch fit his hand well. He had coveted it from the moment he had learned it was in Iroshi's collection. He had fooled her in the choosing as well.

A priest holding one corner of the metal-mesh net stepped into view. Dukane rushed forward, went down on one knee, and cut his legs from under him. The others had followed the first and could not now stop their headlong rush into the corridor.

Two tried to regain control of the net. Before they could, the booreecki had flanked them. Dukane left them to their fun and faced the three who brandished knives.

They surrounded him, Farlow trying to get an opportunity to rush him from the blind side. Dukane turned with them, allowing only a few seconds for any one of them to be at his back. Venting his own, guttural kiai, he rushed toward Farlow, the tallest and strongest, the sword lashing out to knock the knife out of the priest's hands. Swinging the long sword around, he cut the man's head from his shoulders.

The other two took to their heels without looking back once. Screams brought his attention to the other part of the fray.

Sandoval and Vieren ripped at the body of one priest. The last one had disappeared in the opposite direction from his brothers.

Dukane rested the point of his sword on the floor and leaned on it. Blood puddled on the floor. The metal of the weapon vibrated slightly and seemed to moan from the impact. A trick of his imagination, he reasoned, that the sound was so mournful.

Unbridled joy emanated from the booreecki. They had hunted successfully and soon would be sated. He would have to pull them away soon. It was nearly time to seek out Iroshi and her lover.

# 14

❖

Wind howled around the house as if angry that it could find no way inside. A mournful sound, it forced awareness of its existence if not its power, adding to distractions from the day. Iroshi had nearly asked Logan not to come.

Even as they lay together on the immense bed, his caresses could not stop the tumble of thoughts. It was unbelievable in a way that Dukane could have followed from Rune-Nelson, but both she and Ensi had become convinced that the thoughts and images they had received were his and Paige's.

Garon had noticed too, although Erik's sensitivity was not strong enough. The contact had been intense but brief, making it difficult to be sure.

Logan kissed her lightly on the mouth and raised up on one elbow to look down at her.

"Your mind is elsewhere tonight," he said. "Maybe I should go."

No hurt feelings colored the offer, just an acceptance of who she was and what that meant. Iroshi touched his cheek with a fingertip.

"Then you would be a distraction by your absence," she said. "I would hear you in the room next door and keep wishing you were here."

Earlier that evening, Floyd had helped him move his things from the Athenian house. Everything had gone into the second bedroom of the suite, where he had stayed just long enough to unpack and put everything away. Afterward, they had dinner in her sitting room.

"Something's bothering you," she said into a long silence.

He grinned and shook his head. "Not bothering me exactly." He grew more serious. "How much of that scene in the conference hall did you plan?"

She hesitated just long enough for Ensi to confirm what she felt she knew: Logan was not accusing her. He just knew the fight with Pryhs and his death had not been wholly spontaneous and was a little unsure how he felt about it.

"It was clear that Pryhs had to be eliminated, but . . ."

"You think killing him might have been going too far," she finished when he stopped. He nodded. "That was not part of the plan," she said. Although it had always been a distinct possibility, of course, and the one she had preferred. "His arrest would have served almost as well."

*Logan wants to believe that,* Ensi said. *However, he does not quite.*

"Because . . ." she prompted silently.

*He senses it from you and he is beginning to understand how ruthless you can be.*

"Is he sensing your presence?"

*Only vaguely. I was there a bare moment. His thoughts project when he is not on guard.*

"Why isn't he on guard? He's always on guard."

*I think he is inviting you in.*

Now, there was a frightening thought. Inviting her inside his mind, his body, to experience what? Certainly not the same closeness of the other night. A question to consider later. Better to concentrate on the other question, the one concerning Pryhs.

And what more could she tell Logan about him? That the possibility of the man's showing up at the conference on that particular morning was expected? No, more than expected. She had made sure that he got word about Layton's appearance at the meeting. Pryhs knew what that probably meant: his partner was preparing to sell out the principles and action that were so important to him. Anyone who knew Pryhs would also know he would act on that knowledge. Violently, probably. Only because it was the man's nature.

Iroshi looked up to see Logan still staring down at her. The look in his eyes was still one of love. If she told him the whole truth, that light would go out. Or would it? The manner in which he had spoken certainly indicated he was willing to listen, and Ensi had detected no condemnation.

She reached up and brushed his cheek with her hand. He smiled and started to say something, but she cut him off.

"I knew there was a chance there would be a fight," she said. "There always is, particularly with a man like Pryhs. I also knew he was not likely to wait very long to start that fight. He was impatient. When our meeting did come about, he would either be arrested or he would die."

"You were very careful to make sure Layton wasn't the one to fight him."

"Of course. We need to protect Layton's credibility with his people."

"Do you think he will reenter the scene on your side?"

"I don't have a side in this," she said as if quoting a policy statement. "We are here at the request of the Djedian government."

"And you will do almost amything to make sure that side wins."

"Winning is a relative term, my dear," she said, and pushed him onto his back. "In a case like this, we hope that everyone wins."

She leaned over him and kissed him. His response was strong and warm, so she had probably told him no more than what he had already believed or at least come to suspect. Probably no more than he was willing to accept, which was good too.

He put his arms around her and pulled her to him. His body was warm against hers, and young, and strong, matching his response to her kiss. His hands caressed her back toward her shoulders along her sides. She shivered, reveling in the warmth that spread through her body while letting the thrill of his touch chase along every nerve.

Their kisses grew more passionate, both long and short. He ran his long fingers through her hair, moved his hands toward her waist, and rolled her onto her back. Her breath came in short gasps as his hands moved to caress her breasts and her stomach. Suddenly, the sensations of her body were multiplied by the sensations Logan felt in his hands and his own body. His passion was so thoroughly aroused that he projected much of it into her mind to share.

Caught by surprise, she broke off the kiss. A sharp intake of breath. Her back arched. Her fingers stiffened, then curled into fists. Twice the passion engulfed her. She swam in it, tossed about like waves of the sea. In turn, she projected to him, hoping that Ensi would close all the other doors. Thinking of those doors only a moment. Heat, passion, titillation spread throughout her body. It was too much, yet saying "enough" did not occur to her.

Making love on that level had never happened before. She had often wondered what it might be like, but had never taken the chance of letting her defenses down. Nor had there been very many lovers who were capable of telepathy. Logan gave his mind free rein, and she followed suit. Their minds danced back and forth, matching the movement of their tongues. The fire inside built and built with each touch, each feeling shared, until she thought she would explode.

Dukane lay down on his bed, prepared, he thought, for the adventure he sought. Granted, it had been a long time since he had made love with anyone—man or woman—although he relieved the physical pressure with Wessell. She adored him and would do anything he asked. However, sex with her was nearly akin to sex alone since she had become so addicted to meditation. Many times she fell into a sort of slumber every few minutes.

Don't think of her. Think of Iroshi and her young lover. Become one with him. Touch her mind as she thrilled in ecstasy, not knowing it was nearly Dukane's touch rather than the silly boy's.

Paige found them easily and, yes, they were making love. Dukane closed his eyes in order to concentrate his attention. Passion engulfed him immediately. Iroshi's hands caressed his back. The touch of her hands was so exciting. They kissed. Her lips were so soft, her tongue darting into his mouth so warm. She moaned. No, it was Logan. Or was it?

He pressed more tightly against her, their skin touching the full length of their bodies. Their toes tried to intertwine. He ran his fingers through her hair. Or did she run her fingers through his?

It was all wrong! He could not tell whose mind . . . whose body . . .

They moaned and began moving against each other. They rolled over. She was on top now. Wasn't she?

Dukane opened his eyes. He stared into brown eyes. Heavy eyebrows above them. Blond hair. The boy. How in the hell had he gotten into her mind?

Iroshi and Logan gasped at the same time, but she was only slightly aware of that. She pushed him away and sat up.

"Who in gods' names . . . ?" she said.

Logan lay with the heels of his hands pressed against his temples.

"Someone else was there," he said in disbelief. "Who?"

She shook her head, trying to throw off the cobwebs that had dulled her senses.

"You felt it too." To Ensi she said, "Was it Dukane?"

*Yes. Sorry I was not aware of his presence in time to block him out.*

"Not your fault," she said.

Both she and Ensi had erected the barrier in an instant, once they had detected Dukane's presence. The barrier had also pushed Logan out.

"Search for him, quickly," she said to Ensi. "Get Garon to help."

He was gone. Iroshi turned her attention to Logan, who had sat up. He stayed quite still, hands covering his face. She caressed his back.

"It's all right," she said softly, all pretense of having no telepathy gone. "It's an enemy of mine. He used to be a friend."

"For a moment, I was looking into his eyes," Logan said. "Then I saw through his eyes. Feeling his desire for you. It was obscene."

"You felt more than I did," she said. "Tell me."

He lowered his hands and looked over at her.

"It was just impressions. Yet it felt so unhealthy. Obscene, like I said."

"In what way?"

He shook his head and closed his eyes to concentrate. "Such a mixture of strong feelings." He exhaled loudly. "He doesn't love you. It's closer to worship, I think. I got a sense of his wanting to keep you all to himself. Almost to the point of killing you to keep you away from anyone else."

He looked over at her again and smiled. She smiled back and caressed his back again.

"He hates me," she said. "Not much of a surprise, huh?"

She shifted on the bed so that they sat facing each other.

"I wish I could tell you there's nothing to worry about, but that would be a lie. His name is Martin Dukane. He's a former member of the Glaive; one of our more powerful members. I can't tell you much about him yet." She took one of Logan's hands in both of hers. "He is very dangerous. You probably guessed that. But you must work very hard on keeping a barrier up in your mind. You must keep him out at all costs."

Logan shrugged. "I can handle myself all right."

"No. You don't understand. Dukane is one of the most powerful telepaths I've ever known. He is powerful enough that we in the Glaive never knew how unstable he is. His delusions have gone so far that he has proposed that I be set up as an object of worship within the Glaive."

Logan's smile returned as he caressed her cheek. "I could agree with that one," he said. "I already do."

She leaned forward and kissed him. "But you're easy."

"Uh-huh."

"Do you still think you might like to become a member of the Glaive?"

"Yes," he said. "I would like that very much."

"And you want to keep traveling regularly?"

"I'm trained to negotiate."

"That doesn't answer the question."

She had already sensed that he had grown a little tired of the constant moving around. At the same time, he was willing to serve in the Glaive in any honorable capacity.

"No, I guess it doesn't," he said. "I would like to settle down somewhere for a while. The constant moving is getting a bit tiresome. It feels like I've been on the go all my life."

Logan shifted on the bed, bringing Iroshi's attention back to the engrossing activities of moments earlier. Soon, they would talk further about a position for him within the Glaive.

"Where were we a few minutes ago?" she asked. "Before we were interrupted."

"About here."

He pulled her to him and kissed her.

*No luck,* Ensi reported. *Dukane has hidden himself well.*

"Keep watch, both you and Garon," she said. "I don't want any more surprises. We must protect Logan from attack. He's vulnerable."

*We will. At least now we are sure Dukane is here.*

"Yes. But we don't know what he has planned."

Dammit! He had been careless. How could he have been so careless?

Dukane paced his room. He caught a glimpse of himself in the mirror on the wall. His face was flushed, and his eyes were bloodshot from rubbing them. His palms were sweaty, and his heart pounded in his chest.

He looked into the corner of the room. Vieren had moved to lie beside Sandoval. She had felt Dukane's passion, and it had either frightened her or aroused her. He did not care to know which, not enough to seek the answer. At that moment, her eyes were wide and full upon him. Sandoval lay with his muzzle between his forepaws, eyes closed, but the eyeballs moved under them. Either he was dreaming or feigning sleep.

What did they matter? What was important was that he had nearly realized his dream. Or he had come as close as he was likely to come. The problem was that he had been unable to focus on the boy strongly enough to stay in his perspective. He had kept bouncing from one to the other. The intensity of emotion must have been the reason. Nothing like it had ever happened before. So much emotion on so many levels.

*They do know for sure that you are here on Djed, now,* Paige said. Her tone was accusatory.

"We couldn't have kept that secret forever," Dukane said. "Everything should be over in another day or two anyway. I assume Ensi and Garon are trying to find us."

*Yes. I have the barriers full up.*

"Right. The last thing we want is for them to know exactly where we are."

A flash of passion raced through his mind, and his body responded. He moaned.

"Rerun it for me," he said. "The best parts, anyway."

Paige did so. Dukane stood in the middle of the room, eyes closed, his fists clenched at his sides. It was only a moment, such a little time, but he became fully aroused.

"If only there was a way," he said huskily.

*There is none that I can see.*

She was becoming a real naysayer, which was getting tiresome. Ever since they arrived on Djed, she seemed to have taken a negative view of the things he wanted to do.

"If not alive, then perhaps dead." He voiced the sudden thought.

*Dead?*

With her own personal ambitions restarted once she became a part of Dukane, Paige had not balked at hardly anything the host had proposed. Yet suddenly, this and other possibilities were not to her liking.

"Just a desperate thought," Dukane said. "Such a strong desire."

*I hope it is only that.*

"Of course it is. Only that."

But then, he had always planned to dispose of Iroshi's body himself.

# 15

✦

The warehouse was late-night quiet. Even the four guards outside the office made little noise. Well past midnight, Layton guessed as he raised his arms above his head and stretched. So much had happened the day before, and he was still trying to sort it all out. Such a day; may there never be another one like it. Even the afternoon had been unusually busy with contacting members of his group, to ensure their continued loyalty and assuring them, in turn, of his own passion for their cause.

He had always heard that Iroshi was cunning and ruthless. Until that day he would not have believed just how true that was. He would not misjudge her again.

Poor Pryhs seemed to have misjudged everyone. Even himself. Over the afternoon and evening hours, Layton had tried to conjure up sympathy for his erstwhile partner, but without success. Everything should run much more smoothly now that he was out of the way. Iroshi had probably had the same thoughts about him, too. Yes, that woman should be given immense respect and a wide berth.

The difficult part now was to figure out who his friends were. He looked down at the sheet of paper lying on the desktop. Five names were written down, one under the other: Nole, Roman, Iroshi, Cieras, and Pryhs. The last one had a line drawn through it. That left four to choose from. He no longer trusted Nole, so he drew a line through his name. The only thing that might save that partnership, of course, would be Layton's finding Mrs. Nole before the prime minister's enemies did. Unless they were not the ones who took her, but there was no one else.

Cieras's agenda did not include many items that would be of benefit to Djed. Roman he would not trust under any circumstances. His religion was a self-serving one at best. That left only Iroshi's name not crossed out.

It was not very reassuring to know that the head of the Glaive might be the only possible ally he would have in his fight to guarantee Djed's dominance over persea. He was under no illusions about her willingness to sacrifice him or anyone else to what she saw as the best course. On the other hand, she was certainly more experienced in the ways of trade agreements, along with other areas of expertise that could help Djed.

He wadded up the piece of paper and tossed it into the recycler. Seeing his options written down did not help his uneasiness.

A noise out in the warehouse caught his attention. He listened for a moment and was just about to turn back to his desk when someone spoke.

"Who is it?" one of the guards asked. Sounded like Thios. No one answered.

"Stop right there, dammit, or I'll shoot you," the same voice said. This time Layton was sure it was Thios.

He got up from the chair and started toward the back door of the office. Just then, a gun fired. Layton ran to the door.

"What's going on?" he shouted.

"There's someone just come in," Mahr answered. "Thios shot over his head, but he just keeps coming."

Another shot.

"He hit him!"

Layton had reached the two guards. Running footsteps,

and Burnes and Brunell rushed up from the other side. Mahr turned to make sure it was them.

"I don't see anyone," Layton said.

"Over there." Thios indicated straight ahead with the pistol. "He went down."

A slight rustle of sound, and they grew quiet. Layton sent Burnes to turn on the lights. Brunell took his place to the right. There was movement out there somewhere.

There. A form rose from the floor, silhouetted against the faint light at the other end of the warehouse. It started toward them.

"It's him," Mahr said, his voice edged with superstitious fear. "But you got him, Thios."

"I'll get him again, and he won't get up this time."

Thios fired, the report of the M-22 echoing off the walls. The smell of burnt cordite assaulted Layton's nose, and he stifled a sneeze. The figure dropped but in a moment was up and coming at them.

"I don't believe this shit," Thios said. He raised the gun to fire again.

"Wait," Layton ordered.

"Whatta you mean, wait?"

"Just wait. I think I know who that is."

"Who?"

Feet shuffling along the floor was the only sound that followed. Light flooded the building. Walking toward them was a woman, her grey print dress red-stained in two places.

"It's Mrs. Nole," Layton said. Just who he had thought it was. He understood now. She felt no pain, the nervous system was already dead. Even a head shot might not put her down for good.

He started to give the order to try but stopped. Was there any need to destroy this woman? What threat could she possibly be to them, after all?

A diversion. That's what she was. Someone was coming up behind them.

"Burnes. Brunell. Back to the other side!"

The two started off. Mahr and Thios moved toward Mrs. Nole. Mahr took hold of her arm, and she immediately began to struggle. For whatever reason, she would not be held if she could help it.

"Leave her," Layton shouted. "Thios, we need your gun on the other side."

A shout followed a sound akin to a growl. He started into the office for the pistol that was kept in the desk, but remembered that Pryhs had carried it on his last adventure and the police had kept it. He continued through the office and stopped at the opposite doorway. A scream tore through the air. Impossible to tell whose. A crunching sound followed. Another scream.

He resisted the urge to run out and see what was happening. The second urge was to run out the back door and just keep running.

Dammit! He needed that gun. He pulled a long knife from the sheath at his waist, a poor substitute but the only weapon at hand.

He crouched and eased around the door frame into the warehouse. Keeping close to the office wall, he worked his way toward a stack of boxes. Sounds of a struggle came from the other side of those boxes. Thios fired the pistol, but it did not sound like anyone was hit. Then he screamed.

Layton took a deep breath and started moving around the boxes. He got to the next corner and looked around. Two four-legged monstrosities, about the size of very large dogs, tore at two bodies stretched out on the floor. They growled deep in their throats, chewing and tearing at the flesh. Thios sat on his heels, holding his right wrist with his left hand. The right hand was gone, and blood spurted from the wrist.

Mahr lay sprawled on the floor near Thios. He did not move at all.

Standing over this scene was a tall man wearing a long coat. In the dim light of the warehouse, it was difficult to see his face, but Layton would swear that he was smiling at the carnage spread before him. Layton raised the knife to throw it, and the man looked over at him.

"Hel-lo. What have we here?"

Layton tried to bring his arm forward, but his body seemed frozen suddenly. He could breathe, see, feel, but he could not move. Sweat broke out on his forehead, and the man did smile then.

"Vieren, there is another one for you."

One of the beasts raised its head and looked first at the man, then at Layton. It growled and took a step toward him.

*Iroshi!*

She jerked awake. Ensi called her name again.

"What is it?" she asked, still not fully awake.

*Dukane. He is at Layton's warehouse.*

Logan stirred beside her.

"You found him?"

*No. He—or Paige—sent me a message.*

"What is it?" Logan asked groggily. He turned over to face her.

She silenced him with an upraised hand. "A moment," she said aloud, then to Ensi, "What are they doing at the warehouse?"

Ensi hesitated. He wasn't listening or seeking. Instead, he was not sure how to tell her or even if he should tell her. That meant that the event was over and done. They both knew he would tell her in the end, and she waited patiently. He was not being coy. Not this time.

*They have killed them all,* Ensi said at last.

"All who?"

His words both startled and upset her. Did he speak of Layton?

*You are too eager to take responsibility,* Ensi scolded, anticipating her.

"Never mind that. Who is killed?"

*Layton and several of his followers. They were working late.* Another pause; this time Ensi was sorting out the information he was receiving. *Dukane used booreecki.*

"He did bring animals with him. How many?"

*I do not know. All they let through was that the booreecki tore them apart. As if they were hunting.*

Iroshi shuddered. Too often she was being reminded of those nights of hunting when she was an unwilling participant, drawn through the forests of Rune-Nelson by these animals' telepathic abilities.

*No,* Ensi corrected. *I believe Layton is still alive. But just barely. Someone will have to get to him quickly.*

"Have Garon and Erik get medical help there immediately." She turned to Logan. "I have to get to Layton's warehouse. Now. Would you please wake Floyd and Jacob?"

Logan nodded and got out of bed. Before he put on his robe, she was momentarily distracted by the youthful beauty of his body and a sudden fear for his safety. Shaking off the distraction, she climbed out of bed and began dressing. It took only a few minutes to get her uniform on. However, even in that short time, a hundred thoughts and questions plagued her. The worst of them all were those prompted by her fear that she had brought this particular violence to Layton and his people. Perhaps to all of Djed.

"Where is Logan now?" she asked Ensi as she tucked her hair under the fur hat.

*He is on his way to his room to get dressed. He plans to go with us.*

"No, he mustn't."

She grabbed up the coat and her sword from the chair and moved into the sitting room.

*There really is no reason for him not to go. He already understands how you knew something happened.*

She opened the door and stepped into the hall. With a practiced move, she draped the sword belt over her shoulder with one hand, settling the scabbard across her back, then put on the coat.

She closed the door behind her and paused. This sudden apprehension was more intuition than just concern for someone she cared about. Logan's door opened and he stepped out, still putting on his coat. For the first time, he wore a sword, a French cavalry saber from Earth, plain but expensive.

"I'm ready," he said.

"You know how to use that?"

He looked down at the hilt at his waist, then looked her full in the face.

"Quite well. I've trained since I was a boy."

"Good," she said, and smiled slightly. Maybe he was a warrior after all.

Protesting would waste time, and it was very clear that he did not intend staying behind. Instead, she nodded and he followed her down the stairs. Erik came from the great room to join them at the door. He glanced at Logan with a raised eyebrow but said nothing about his presence.

"Floyd and Jacob are at the car," he said. "Medical help is on the way to the warehouse."

"All right," Iroshi said. "Let's go."

Erik opened the door, and they stepped into the frigid early morning. Light pollution was very low on Djed, and the stars in the black sky were so thickly clustered that they formed grey streaks. Snow sparkled on either side of the heated sidewalk. Except for the low rumble of the car engine, the world was silent.

No one said a word as they climbed into the car, whether out of respect for the silence around them or for the dead they were about to meet, who could say. Maybe they were all too sleepy and stunned.

Jacob guided the car into the street, testing possible slickness. The road surface was heated from beneath, just as the sidewalks were, and the tires gained good traction even on the wet pavement. As the car gained speed, buildings and trees flashed past the windows, all of them dark silhouettes lighted briefly by the headlights.

Iroshi tried not to speculate on what they would find in the warehouse. Ensi sought contact with Dukane, and Garon sought further signs of life among the victims. It was impossible to avoid speculation on the reasons for the slaughter. That Dukane had followed her was not surprising, although she had not expected that he would when they left Rune-Nelson. Figuring out why he would kill Layton and his followers was more difficult to comprehend. And why had he let Ensi know what he had done?

The way in which she had encountered the booreecki was no secret within the Glaive. That had been their first taste of the animals and their telepathic abilities. It had been a nearly disastrous first encounter, and she and Erik and his brother Mark had suffered intensely from the invasion of their minds. Was the use of the animals Dukane's way of trying to intimidate her and Erik? If it was, he had erred seriously. Although the memory was still unpleasant for both of them, neither of them feared the carnivores— they had both taken a large role in raising the two pups they took to Rune-Nevas and in reintroducing them to their home planet. A long search had taken place before others of their kind were found on Rune-Nelson. If they had not been found, attempts to clone would have been the next step.

All that aside, Dukane's motives were still more than a

little unclear. That made anticipating his next move nearly impossible.

Jacob slowed the car and guided it into the parking lot of the warehouse. Darkness enclosed the building. No sign of an ambulance or emergency medical vehicle yet. Erik and Floyd looked at Iroshi; Erik nodded, and the two of them stepped out of the car and drew their weapons: Erik his sword, Floyd a laser pistol. Jacob kept the motor running. Logan started to get out too, but she placed her hand on his arm.

"They know what they're doing," she said softly. "Wait until they check it out."

The two men disappeared into darkness outside the range of the headlights, both moving toward the building. After several minutes, lights came on both outside and inside. Erik appeared at the door of the warehouse and waved to them. Jacob cut the engine, and the three of them got out. Since Erik had sheathed his sword, the situation was clearly safe for the moment.

Logan and Floyd flanked Iroshi as she made her way across the snowy surface. Erik held the door open for them.

"Layton?" she asked.

"Still alive."

They filed past Erik, and he brought up the rear. Their footsteps echoed through the nearly empty interior, sounding more eerie than the first time. Someone groaned in the distance, a soft sound without any strength behind it. The smell of blood came faintly. Rounding a pile of crates, she came upon the scene and stopped dead in her tracks.

At first, she saw only Layton being looked over by Floyd. His groans were more audible now, but only a little. He and his clothes were one bloody mass. Two other bodies lay close by, neither as brutalized as Layton, but neither of them moved. Their attitudes, unnaturally twisted, be-

# PERSEA 163

spoke unconsciousness if not death. All three lay in dark pools of their own blood.

"There are two more over there," Erik said, pointing toward the other side of the office. "All dead."

"The same way?" Iroshi asked.

"Worse. They were partially eaten."

She could not suppress the shudder that shook her body. Logan placed a hand on her arm, but she ignored it.

"Ensi," she called silently. "Can Layton live?"

*It will take a supreme effort and only if the medical people get here soon,* he said. *Shock and the loss of blood are overpowering.*

"I feel it," she said. "Do what you can to ease his pain."

*Look to Logan,* Ensi warned.

She turned and found the younger man had taken a few steps away from her. His face was drained of all color. His left hand, which he held flat against his chest, trembled uncontrollably. The hand she had thought he had placed on her arm to reassure her was balled into a fist. She stepped close to him, took hold of his right hand gripping her arm, and squeezed it. He looked down at her, but his eyes did not focus on her. His nostrils flared, and he swallowed hard.

"Logan," she said. "Will you go outside and watch for the medics, please?"

It was another second before he could focus on her face. He swallowed again and nodded. He walked away, his back ramrod straight, his shoulders squared, unhurried but with a sense of relief that she felt strongly. She was tempted to go with him. Instead, she turned toward Layton.

He no longer groaned in pain; Ensi's magic was working. Even so, the smell of death hovered near him. If only that damned ambulance would hurry.

Vieren lay on the floor of the back seat beside his feet,

washing herself with great relish. Dukane was now her special friend again; he had allowed her and her mate to hunt, to feel the fear that was every bit as much nourishment as were the meat and blood, so warm and fresh.

Their pleasure and satiation filled Dukane, satisfying him even more than had his own meal or having sex with Wessell. Almost as much as eavesdropping on Iroshi's sex with her young lover. The little bit of human flesh he included in their regular food had given them such an appreciation for that particualr meat. Their love of the hunt had done the rest. Only these two, of all the booreecki, had been specially trained by him. They appreciated their special place in his world. Or else.

*They are at the warehouse,* Paige said.

"Careful," Dukane said. "Don't let them feel you."

*Of course not,* she said with more than a touch of exasperation.

The companion had gotten even more irritable over the last day or so. The strain was telling on her. Perhaps events should be slowed a bit to let her catch her breath, so to speak.

However, there was no time for such niceties. Everything had been set in motion, and they could not slow down now. They must keep Iroshi and her followers off balance from here on. One disaster after another until the final eruption of violence and cleansing.

*The time has come,* Paige said.

They had discussed the timing for this particular final moment. He turned inward and linked with Paige, letting himself be pulled along. The car sped on as they entered Layton's mind together. Dukane reached out his hand and crushed the mind that lay wounded and vulnerable.

# 16

✦✧

She had just started to kneel beside the stricken man when he screamed in terror and pain. Ensi gasped, rushing back into her mind with such suddenness that she gasped in turn. Layton shuddered, his eyes snapped open, then he stiffened and died.

Everything went black as she and Ensi felt him die. Her knees buckled. It lasted only a moment, but when she could see again, she found Erik and Logan on either side, supporting her, looks of concern on both faces.

Ensi had also recovered his equilibrium, although he was clearly shaken.

*He was aware of what was happening in spite of being unconscious,* he said. *It was very much like a nightmare for him.*

"I know," she said silently. Aloud she said, "He's not finished."

"Who?" Erik asked.

"Dukane." She straightened, and they both released their hold on her. When did Logan come back into the warehouse? "We have to hurry. He's going after the Noles."

"Right now?" Erik asked.

"The Noles?" Logan said. "You mean Prime Minister Nole."

"Him and his wife," Iroshi explained. "And yes, now. I think Dukane is the one who took her from Layton and his people."

Behind Logan, she saw med techs checking out the bodies, all of whom were now dead.

"But she's away in the country," Logan said.

"Never was," Erik said.

"Floyd," Iroshi called. "Stay here. Try to get hold of Nole or Yenson with the palace guards. Warn them about Dukane and the booreecki." She turned toward the door. "Let's go."

Jacob was out the door and had the car started by the time they reached it. In moments they were speeding along the streets. Greater darkness fell upon the city as the few lights went out.

"Hurry," she said.

Iroshi wondered if the sun would ever shine here again.

Cline had been successful in his assignment, and getting into the palace had been easy. In the darkness brought on by the sabotage of the power station, the guards saw the Patriarch's official car, with banners and pennants fluttering from every fender, and waved him through. Not once did anyone look inside the car to make sure it was actually the Patriarch sitting in the back seat.

Now Dukane led Mrs. Nole along the corridors where emergency lights did little to brighten the way. The dark stains of dried blood on her dress were merely darker shadows. The loss of blood had weakened her, and she stumbled frequently.

Vieren and Sandoval followed close behind. In spite of their feeding at the warehouse, the two were still hungry. He had dragged them away to guarantee that they would not only still be hungry but also in an eager mood.

He stopped the lifeless woman at the entrance to the suite she once shared with her husband. Nole lay asleep inside, oblivious to his visitors. He tossed and turned in the bed, plagued by dreams that often featured Mrs. Nole at their center.

Paige returned from searching the room and its occupant. The companion was ill at ease.

*Let's leave this for later,* she said. *Iroshi and the others are on their way, and the guards will soon be alerted.*

"We'll never have a better opportunity," Dukane said. "We'll finish it now."

With one swift kick, the door was battered open.

*It might have been unlocked,* Paige said testily.

"Like you said, there isn't much time."

Nole's voice shouted from the bedroom, demanding to know what the hell was going on. Dukane marched through the sitting room, nearly dragging the helpless woman. Vieren and Sandoval growled, their own tension heightened by the crashing of the door.

An emergency light shone in the bedroom when the bizarre party walked in. Nole was up and nearly had his robe on.

"Who the hell are you?" he demanded. He squinted at them, trying to get a clear look.

"I brought you something," Dukane said.

He pulled Mrs. Nole around in front of him, then shoved her onto the bed. She fell into the shaft of light that bisected it and did not move. Silence had fallen over them all as even the carnivores looked at her still form. She blinked.

"Lisley," Nole said.

His expression was a mixture of fear and love. Dukane suddenly realized that look mirrored his own feelings for Iroshi. The combination was powerful, nearly debilitating, and that was why he had to crush her. Then he could rebuild her in the proper image and save himself from his own desires. Mrs. Nole, however, was beyond repair.

*He wants to go to her but is afraid.*

"He's been afraid all his life."

Nole looked from his wife to Dukane.

"What do you want?" he asked.

"Nothing from you. You are no more than a pawn in the game."

"Then why are you here?"

"Iroshi."

"What? You know her?"

"She is my god, and you will be sacrificed on her altar. She must be made to understand her place."

"That's ridiculous."

Dukane shrugged and smiled. "It will sound good to some. Too bad you couldn't enjoy it. There will be little else for you to hear."

Vieren and Sandoval growled as he mentally released them. Neither of them paid any attention to the woman lying on the bed. Her body was cold, she was dead, and, unless ordered to do so, they did not consider her game. The man on the other side of the bed was different. He moved and made noises, and now fear exuded from every pore.

Cornered, Nole punched buttons on the console next to his bed as the two animals closed in.

Iroshi and her people hurried through the corridors of the palace, led by three of the palace guards who had met them at the main entrance. Torches and emergency lights lit their way. She hurried even though she knew it was too late. Ensi had sought out the prime minister as the car rushed through dark streets. They had both felt his fear and horror when the two booreecki rushed at him. They heard both their growls and his screams; through his eyes and ears they watched and felt the carnivores tear at his flesh. In an instant Iroshi had closed down. She had seen too much already.

How in the hell were they going to stop Dukane? They had to find a way, and soon.

Everyone slowed as they neared the suite. The now familiar smell of blood tainted the air, but no one moaned in the rooms beyond. One of the guards went in first. In a few minutes, his exclamations of horror could be heard clearly. Yenson, who had gotten there ahead of them, appeared after a few minutes.

"It's safe to go in," he said, "but I don't think you want to."

"Is Mrs. Nole in there?" Iroshi asked.

"Yes. She has been shot and is comatose. She's lying on the bed, her eyes are open, but we couldn't rouse her at all. No wonder, after being shot and perhaps seeing what happened to her husband. Funny thing, I didn't know she was back in the palace."

Iroshi and Erik exchanged glances and Logan watched both of them. There had been no time on the way from the warehouse to explain to him about Lisley Nole or certain effects of the formula.

Lord, that was one thing that had been lost sight of during all the recent events. Not many days ago, persea had been the one abiding item of interest for them all. Now there were more immediate matters to tend to.

"I'll go in and check on everything," Erik said.

She nodded as more guards appeared. Major Yenson had readily accepted the Glaive's presence. His prime minister, and direct superior, was dead. He was a competent police officer, but this sort of event had never happened during his career. The government itself would take time to sort it all out, appoint an interim leader, and direct the investigation. Too much time, he was thinking, and having Iroshi ready to step in now helped him maintain his composure.

"Major, could we start checking into who came to and went from the palace tonight? I assume there is a log of visitors and perhaps even holo cameras at the entrances and exits."

"We can check all of that in the command center," he said, and led the way.

He continued talking, describing the equipment they had recently installed, most of it the latest technology. The new installations were necessary, given the volatility of events associated with persea and the influx of important visitors. However, Iroshi listened with only half an ear.

"No signs of Dukane?" she asked Ensi after he had completed a sweep of the palace.

*None. He could still be here, of course.*

"What about the booreecki? Couldn't we detect them more easily?"

*I have scanned for them too. The training we gave them to suppress their transference may also keep them from being detected. It is very much like the shield that Dukane uses.*

The possibility of someone using the carnivores against anyone in the Glaive had never been foreseen. Although the possibility of a rogue like Dukane had been foreseen, that had not helped them avoid the problem. If she kept reminding herself that they were only human, and that they made mistakes in judgment like anyone else, it was easier to focus on the problems rather than blaming herself. Something that Ensi constantly reminded her to do.

"Here we are," Yenson said, stopping in front of a door.

They had moved from the second level to the first level. Inside, the room was large and spacious in spite of the tons of equipment housed there. Several holo screens showed various parts of the palace, both the grounds and inside the building. As the scenes changed over and over, the three guards sitting in front of the screens had a view of most of the palace complex.

A fourth man, a captain by his insignia, left his desk to the right and approached Yenson.

"Is it true, Major?" he asked.

"Yes, Vincenn, it's true. The prime minister is dead."

The captain stiffened slightly and exhaled a little loudly. The three men, sitting with their backs to the door, showed little physical reaction. The one on the left closed his hand into a fist on top of the console where he sat. Even with so little overt reaction, the tension in the room increased. They were responsible for protecting the complex and its occupants, and they had failed. Even though part of that failure—the power outage—had been beyond their control, a strong desire to rectify that failure emanated from each one.

"I need to see the entry and exit log for tonight," Yenson continued.

"Yes, sir."

Vincenn stepped to one of the consoles and removed a comm cube. He inserted it into a handheld viewer which he gave to his superior. Yenson held the viewer so both he and Iroshi could see it. The pictures were not very clear, since the main lights had been out at that time. Meanwhile, Ensi probed each of the four men, looking for whatever they might have seen over and above the recorded events.

"Whose vehicle is that?" Iroshi asked as she pointed at the screen.

It was a very large car with numerous banners and pennants flying from the fenders. The windows were dark, and no occupants could be seen at all.

"That's the Patriarch's," Yenson answered.

"What time?"

He touched a pad on the viewer and the time lit up.

"Almost an hour ago," Iroshi mused. She looked at the captain. "Did anyone check to make sure that it was Roman inside that car and not someone else?"

"No," he answered immediately. "No one stops the Patriarch. He comes and goes at will."

"Any indication of whom he saw while he was here?"

"None," Yenson said. "He often checks on the chapel here, and there are two priests. He confers with officials on government and church matters. It could have been anyone."

"Or it could have been someone else in that car," Iroshi said. "When did it leave?"

The captain consulted the log, and Yenson searched through the holo record.

"He hasn't," Yenson said first.

"Find that car!" Iroshi said.

"But . . ."

"That car would be the easiest way for our killer to have gained entrance to the Palace."

The two officers looked at each other, and Yenson nodded to the captain but refused to meet her gaze.

"What's the matter, Major?"

"From the way Nole's body was ripped apart, that had to be an animal, not a person."

"Don't you think that a person could make an animal do such a thing? What kind of animal do you have here on Djed that could or would kill a person that way? Particularly, what kind could get inside this building in order to do it?"

She knew the answer as well as he did. Djed was home to very few wild animals. Even fewer of those were carnivores, and of those, only one had the teeth or claws capable of actually ripping a person apart. However, it was not native to this part of Djed. The killer had to have come from off-world.

Vincenn, who had moved to the comm console, was issuing orders. The major was not quite ready to accept her argument.

"You agree that it was an animal that killed Nole?" he asked. Iroshi nodded. "Where did this animal come from? How did it get here without anyone knowing?"

"Do you have no smugglers on Djed, Major?"

"Of course we do."

"That means there must be landing fields and other arrangements which make it possible for the smugglers to get their goods dirtside. Frankly, I wouldn't be at all surprised if Roman doesn't know of a few himself."

"The Patriarch is the head of our most important religious order," Yenson said stiffly.

"I'm sorry, Major. I meant no offense. It's just that I've seen so many things on other worlds. Perhaps you are right and I'm just too jaded by past experience."

"The car has been found," Vincenn reported.

"Where?" Yenson asked.

"In one of the garage areas."

"Anyone in it?"

"They're checking now."

They all waited in silence. The screens flickered from one scene to another. Ensi still searched the palace in his own way, hoping for just one sign of Dukane. They both knew that if the car was still here, Dukane and his booreecki might be too. That could mean a chance of capturing him, or a chance that he would let his animals kill again, or both.

The minutes stretched out. The guards must be approaching the vehicle very carefully. At last Vincenn blinked and turned toward them.

"Only one occupant," he reported. "The driver. His throat's been cut."

"Major," Iroshi said. "I would strongly suggest that you have your men check on your Patriarch to make sure he isn't dead too."

# 17

✦

"Of course I'm not dead," Roman said loudly. "Whatever made you ask such a question?"

He was too cheerful, trying too hard to convince them that everything was all right. Yenson began explaining what had happened at the palace and the role the Patriarch's car had seemingly played in the tragedy.

*He is lying,* Ensi confirmed, having gone beyond the usual scanning under the circumstances. *He has been sheltering Dukane and a couple of his followers. Mrs. Nole too, it would seem. He did not know, however, that Dukane had taken his official car or his driver. His Holiness is afraid.*

"He should be afraid. Does he have any idea where Dukane is at this moment?"

*None. Right now he wants as little to do with Dukane as possible.*

"Would Dukane be able to shield Roman's thoughts from us?"

Ensi took his time answering that question. Dukane and the depth of his abilities had come as a surprise to everyone. That Ensi might know about this particular aspect was unlikely. Still, it was a logical next question.

*It is possible,* Ensi said at last. *It is not possible to know for sure. Not until we encounter him doing just that. We would at least know when it happens.*

Yes, at least that much. For now, Roman raved over the attack on the prime minister and his wife, honestly appalled at the manner in which Nole died. Yenson managed to get off the line in short order, in spite of the Patriarch's obvious desire to know more. He motioned for Iroshi to follow him into his office just off the main room. The muscle in his right jaw twitched visibly.

He walked around the desk placed in the exact center of the office and sat down in his chair. He leaned back with a sigh that did not relieve the tension he clearly felt. Iroshi took one of the two chairs opposite, Logan the other. Although he had not actually been invited in, she had not discouraged his tagging along.

"Now," Yenson began. "There are some things you know that you haven't told me. Aren't there?"

She shrugged. "Like what, Major?"

"I think you know who our killer is."

"I do. Or at least, have every reason to think I do." When she paused, Yenson did not prompt her to continue. In a moment she went on anyway, having resolved that she must do so in order to protect any other possible target.

"His name is Martin Dukane. He is a member of the Glaive. We believe that he has two booreecki with him, carnivores from Rune-Nelson. These animals live for one thing, for the most part: to hunt. It would seem that he is using them as weapons for killing people. It was the same way he killed Layton and his followers earlier tonight in the warehouse they used as headquarters."

"Layton is dead?"

"I'm afraid so."

Yenson shook his head in disbelief.

"Why is this Dukane doing all this?"

"Revenge. I removed him from a job that had become too important to him, and he believes that I betrayed him."

"So, this trouble followed you here and has nothing to do with Djed."

"Correct. At least nothing to do with Djed until now."

Yenson tented his fingers and looked past her at the wall for a moment. He shifted his eyes back toward her.

"Any suggestions on how we can capture this Dukane and his pets?"

Thank goodness the major was a pragmatist. Many others in his present position would be throwing accusations about instead of looking for solutions.

"I would first suggest very strongly that you provide the Patriarch with an armed guard. Since Dukane used his car, there might be reason to believe that he would return to the temple. Next, provide protection for all of the principals involved in the negotiations concerning the formula. Dukane seems to be marking them for execution in order to throw me off guard, or perhaps to soil my or the Glaive's reputation."

Yenson nodded. "If you left, would he follow you?"

"Probably not right away, but I have no way of knowing that for sure."

She waited for him to ask her to leave Djed just in case she was wrong about his good sense. He certainly did not want anyone else dying on his world and, if he was as smart as she thought he was, he would consider her absence one very good way of not having to deal with any part of this. Send it somewhere else, for someone else to handle. If he did ask, what choice would she have? Dealing with Dukane here and now would be more to her liking. However, this was Yenson's world, not hers or the Glaive's. To what world would it be best to try to lead Dukane? She stopped speculating on that as Yenson broke the silence.

"We will do all that we can to help. I suspect that you're right about his not following you right away. I haven't had much experience with the killer mind, but this one seems bent on embarrassing you. If you left and he didn't follow, that would prove most embarrassing to us all."

This was a brave man facing her. And a farsighted one. It

was time to tell him everything she could, then, to maximize their new cooperation. Logan, sitting beside her, could get it all at the same time. Later she would tell him even more.

It was full daylight by the time she and her people left the palace. In spite of the best efforts of Yenson's guards, Dukane had not been found within its confines. Ensi confirmed that Roman had no idea where the renegade was. The Patriarch was still frightened, although guards surrounded the temple. He had good reason to be.

Logan was quiet on the ride back to the house. They had only a short time to talk, get some sleep, and be back at the conference hall. A meeting had been scheduled to dicuss how to proceed now that Nole was dead. First, though, she wanted Logan to understand about Lisley Nole and persea, and she told him everything she knew and suspected.

They arrived at the house, and everyone went to their respective rooms. Logan promised to meet her in her room as soon as he had finished his shower. She had just turned off her own shower when she heard him come into the bedroom. She wrapped her robe around herself and stepped out of the bathroom. Logan sat in one of the easy chairs, his head back and his eyes closed. He knew she was in the room, but he was so tired.

"Would you prefer we talk later?" she asked.

He opened his eyes and smiled. "No, now is all right."

He held out his hand to her and she took it in her own.

"I know that you have secrets," he said. "But I would like to think that you and I are a little closer than many other people you know."

"We are," she assured him. "The closer you get to becoming a member of the Glaive, the more I can reveal about myself and the guild."

"I don't mean just that," he said.

"I know."

She squeezed his hand and sat in the chair across from him. Turning the reference from their personal relationship to a more professional one was deliberate.

"You've been very patient," Iroshi said, "and I appreciate that. I know, too, that you understand more than most people would because of your special talents."

She stretched with her arms overhead and legs extended in front of her. Gods, she was tired and needed some sleep. Logan would probably accept it if she decided not to tell him all just now, but that would not be fair since she had come this far. He was too keyed up to sleep soon, just as she was, and it was just as well to get this done now rather than later.

"I guess one of the first things you would like to know about is Mrs. Nole. I believe I told you she was dying from Philella's fever. From what we've learned, she actually died several weeks ago."

She went on to describe how the formula had been administered to Mrs. Nole at the moment of death and how it had revived her body but not her mind. She started to add "soul," but that seemed out of her rights to decide. She also told him everything they had learned about the others treated in the same way.

He listened intently and Ensi probed his reactions, at least on the surface. Even she could sense that not all of this came as a surprise to him, although he had not understood everything before. He was surprised when she told him that Nole had secretly headed the group supposedly led by Layton.

"He must have been terribly unsettled by what happened to his wife," Logan commented.

"Yes, he was. The desire to discredit and ruin Doctor Drace overcame his original goal of bringing Djed into the mainstream with persea. There was a very strong feeling that he was tearing himself in two."

She yawned and put her head back, closing her eyes. The dampness of the robe was beginning to chill her.

"The Glaive determined that negating any power Layton's organization had would be the best way in which to handle him?" Logan asked.

"Yes. That was why we drew Layton to our side."

"And why you allowed Pryhs to pick a fight with you."

Iroshi did not look up. She knew that he had figured that out, of course. The fear that he would condemn her for manipulating a man to his death returned, but Ensi assured her that he had no such feelings. He was a very pragmatic man, after all, and recognized that some steps might be as distasteful as they were necessary. He understood power and its uses.

"I accepted that he would probably make that choice rather than trying to reason with me," she said. "He and Layton made a good team, if they had only realized it. There was a good balance between their personalities. Too bad for them that they fought each other rather than figuring out how to cooperate."

"Nole may have been the factor that would prevent that from ever happening."

"Quite possibly. I think he would have torn this whole world apart if he'd had his way. In the end, the Glaive's being here actually worked against his aims. He wanted them all fighting against each other, and we were trying to get them to cooperate."

Logan yawned and stretched. "What do you think everyone will want to do now?"

"Cieras will want the negotiations to continue, of course," she said after some thought. "She may be mad as hell at you, but she needs to succeed to preserve her career. This thing has gone on too long with no end in sight."

Logan agreed, and they talked a short while longer about what might be decided in the meeting later in the day. Talk dried up from sheer exhaustion, and when she found herself nodding off, she sent Logan to his room to sleep and crawled into bed by herself. She lay for a time worrying about the one thing that she could not tell Logan: how to protect herself and Ensi from intrusion by the booreecki. So much had been learned about their telepathic abilities, and ways to block their transference had been perfected. Except those ways depended in part on the training the animals were given. These two had been trained by Dukane.

She drifted off to sleep, dreamless and deep. Sometime later, she woke with a start.

"Who . . . ?"

*I do not know,* Ensi said. *Someone or something tried to scan your mind.*

Fear spawned by old memories raced up and down her spine. She turned onto her back.

"Logan?"

*No, it was not him.*

"I meant, is he all right? Did anyone try to scan him?"

*I do not think so. Dukane probably does not even know that he is telepathic.*

"That may be his salvation. It was Dukane or the booreecki who intruded, then?"

*Contact did not last long enough to tell.*

"Anything happening with the Patriarch?"

*No. I scan for him continuously but have detected no immediate danger. He has not slept all night.*

"He's the lucky one, anyway," Iroshi said. "He has no real idea what he's afraid of."

She drifted back into sleep in spite of the fear that still peeked into every corner of her mind. Ensi built walls and stayed alert.

The conference room was quiet. Everyone was there who had been invited. Yenson was there, not only as head of security, but also as Nole's replacement. No one else in the government had been eager to replace the prime minister, not even Sair Allala, second in the government, who was attending her first meeting. She sat next to Yenson, not quite frightened enough to give up all say in the matter, and the two talked in low voices, discussing some last-minute thoughts on the day's activities.

Yenson looked as tired as Iroshi felt. He had supervised most of the guard and police activities during the night and had gotten almost no sleep.

Cieras was unusually quiet, casting looks of hate toward Iroshi and Logan every once in a while. Others had questioned his sudden switch in loyalty, but only among themselves. He had been replaced by one of the other members of her team. Two other members of the Athenian delegation were also in attendance.

Dr. Drace kept looking at Iroshi also, wondering how much she knew about Mrs. Nole and her condition. She felt her whole world, all of her ambition, and her chance for fame and fortune about to disappear forever. Two doctors from her research team flanked her, worried expressions on their faces, too.

Iroshi had set Ensi to gathering all the information Drace had on the formula, not willing to believe that everything was recorded. No matter what happened to any of them, she wanted that information to be saved. They might not be able to get it out to the marketplace soon, but they would one day.

Erik sat on her other side, alert and worried in his own way. He, too, had been scanned momentarily during the night, which had put him on edge. Garon kept watch for any sign of Dukane or the carnivores. As usual, Floyd and Jacob sat behind her in chairs against the wall. She felt safe from attack except from within and, even there, everything had been done that could be to protect her and Erik.

Although Logan was telepathic, he had less to worry about regarding a direct attack if Dukane had not realized he had that talent. Only the booreecki might endanger him.

A tense group, meeting to decide where these negotiations would go next. Or if they would even continue at this stage. The overall impression was that everyone wanted to go on. No one was sure that they could.

Guards stood around the perimeter of the room and outside in the foyer, all armed with laser rifles. They had been warned to watch for Dukane and had been given a description of him and the booreecki. Iroshi suspected that the animals would be the ones to show up. Dukane had too many plans to risk his own safety.

Try as they might, none from the Glaive had any more chance of detecting the enemy's presence than anyone else did. The first signal might come from the guards posted outside when they reacted to an attack or sudden appearance.

Yenson looked around the table and cleared his throat.

"We might as well get started," he said. "The first order of business, of course, is to discuss whether or not we should continue with these negotiations."

"Of course we should continue," Cieras said loudly. She felt for the grip of the knife at her belt. Everyone had come armed with knives and swords. "We have too much time and money invested in this matter to give up now."

"Since you're so eager to talk, please continue, Madam Cieras," Yenson said. His exhaustion showed in his impatience with the Athenian.

"I just want to make it known that not continuing is not an option as far as we are concerned," she said petulantly. "Dropping the whole deal should not even be considered just because your prime minister has been killed."

"It isn't just because Prime Minister Nole was killed, Madam," Yenson said. "There is the added consideration that all of you may be in danger. More than one person has been killed, as you know. Burgh Layton was also killed last night."

Cieras snorted and waved her hand, as if that death had no importance.

"It is believed these deaths—several of Layton's followers were also killed—are connected. Because both Layton and Nole were involved in the matter before us, that would appear to be a logical assumption."

"Nonsense," Cieras said. "Even if that were true, surely there are enough guards here to protect us from any danger." She looked at Iroshi and pointed. "Is this your idea, Iroshi of the Glaive?"

"I have no say in the decisions of the government of Djed," Iroshi said. "I admit to having consulted with Major Yenson last night, but whatever decision is reached here today will be an outcome of today's discussions, not of what the two of us discussed."

"All I can say is, if you haven't the nerve to stick it out, you had best leave this to professionals."

Iroshi laughed at the attempted insult. Everyone in the room knew that the Glaive and its leader had more experience than Cieras could ever hope to have. Such a blunder could only be prompted by a bad case of nerves. Cieras's face turned red and she sputtered, unable to get any words out.

"I beg your pardon, Madam," Iroshi said. "I know you would not have said such a thing if you weren't under so much stress. As we all are." She turned away from Cieras and faced Yenson once more. "I apologize to you also, for perhaps speaking out of turn."

The major nodded, a bit of a smile touching the corners of his mouth.

"Dr. Drace," he said, "what is your feeling in this matter?"

Drace cleared her throat and made as if to get to her feet,

then thought better of it. Instead, she leaned forward self-consciously.

"I must admit," she said, "there have been times during the past few days that I have almost wished we had never discovered the formula. So far, it has not been the boon to humanity I—we—had envisioned." She twirled the gold ring on her finger. "However, in the cold light of day—of this day in particular—I don't think we have any choice but to go on. To take our chances, in a manner of speaking."

"Right!" Cieras interjected. Yenson glared at her, and she said no more.

"Anyway, I believe that we should proceed as Nole originally intended," Drace went on.

*She is afraid of what might come out now that Lisley Nole is on the loose,"* Ensi said.

"She needn't worry," Iroshi answered. "Everyone believes Mrs. Nole has been traumatized by her husband's death and her own wounds."

*Drace does not quite believe that. She wonders why she was not summoned last night to care for the prime minister's wife.*

"I believe there was some notion that Drace was in the country. Anyway, she'll get over it. We don't want to see her ruined just yet. Not until we're certain we have all we need to duplicate persea."

Drace sat back in her chair and continued to twist the ring on her finger. An awkward silence fell over the gathering, and Iroshi looked from face to face. Every one of them was frightened or unsure of him or herself. Except Yenson, who was just plain tired.

"Give Yenson a nudge," she told Ensi.

Ensi planted an instantaneous suggestion that Iroshi should be given a chance to speak now. The major looked her way and nodded.

"Iroshi, your turn to tell us what you believe we should do."

"At this juncture it would seem only politic to agree with my counterparts in this affair. I believe that we should pursue agreement on the issues originally put before us all. However, we cannot proceed without the cooperation of the Djedian government. How do you vote, Major Yenson?"

He smiled once again.

"Having only recently become a spokesman for my government . . ."

A loud commotion erupted in the foyer. Shots were fired. Growls followed by screams of pain.

*The booreecki,* Ensi said, a little late.

# 18

❖

The car sat two blocks from the conference hall, the engine off, everything quiet inside and out. It was another vehicle belonging to the temple, and the Patriarch had no idea that Dukane had it. Dukane sat behind the wheel, eyes closed, listening, watching, as events unfolded in the building down the street.

Once inside, the two booreecki had begun transmitting back to him, letting him see and hear everything that happened. The scenes were only a little distorted by the animals' own perceptions.

Four guards stood outside the actual conference room, all armed and ready. Yet they were caught by surprise when the small explosive packet Dukane had placed there destroyed the double doors. Vieren and Sandoval pushed through the smoke and debris. They attacked two of the guards at once, before they had a chance to level their rifles. One of the remaining two managed to hit Vieren in the side before Sandoval was on him. The beam glanced off the harness she wore, only slightly grazing her side. She was back on her feet in seconds. The last guard fired several times but was too excited to aim well. He screamed as he went down.

Dukane guided his two pets to the correct door, instructing them on how to open it. They rushed inside, dodged the guards in there, and got under the table. Both growled, letting the two-legged ones know not to mess with them.

"Lie down," Dukane ordered, and they did.

He fingered the small control box that linked to the pack on Vieren's back. Sandoval would stick close to her, convinced that he must protect his mate and the burden she carried.

Not yet. Not yet. How long should he wait? The feelings of fear and confusion he got both directly and indirectly through the booreecki were intoxicating.

*Get it over with,* Paige said. *The longer you hesitate, the better the chance we will be found.*

"Dammit. Can't you just enjoy the feelings? Why are you losing your nerve?"

*You take too many chances. Take too much pleasure in the steps necessary to achieve the goal. It is the goal that should bring pleasure.*

"And what do you consider the goal to be?"

They were coming apart; their mutual enthusiasm had waned. If their ultimate goal was no longer the same, steps must be taken now to bring their actions and aims back in line.

*Iroshi, of course. We must set her up as the goddess of the Glaive. We must keep her from ruining her reputation. We must enhance . . .*

"All right, Paige. We have the same aims. The same devotion to the image of Iroshi. Stop worrying about how we get there. I'll take care of that."

Dukane turned his attention back to the touch pad on the control box. One thing he would regret was not having another chance to eavesdrop or, even better, to participate directly in a romantic interlude with her. But he could play with her a little.

"What does that creature have on its back?" Yenson asked.

Everyone had moved away from the table the moment

the booreecki went under it. For the moment they stood perfectly still, not quite sure what might happen next.

"I'd say it's a bomb, Major," Logan said.

*If anyone tries to leave the room, I will detonate it,* Dukane's voice said in Iroshi's head. Ensi had let the pronouncement through as it was fed through the carnivores.

"A bomb!" Cieras shouted. "Let's get the hell out of here."

"Stop!" Iroshi did not raise her voice, but her tone halted everyone in their tracks. "Don't move. Any of you."

She looked at Logan, who nodded. He had heard the same warning. Very slowly, she moved close to Yenson; all the while the animals kept their eyes on her. It wasn't their reaction that she feared at the moment.

"The bomb will be detonated if anyone tries to leave the room," she told the major softly. "No doubt it will be detonated sooner or later, regardless, but it would be wise to buy as much time as we can."

Cieras took a step toward the nearest door, and the female animal turned to look at her. The Athenian stopped, the fear in her eyes increasing every moment. Iroshi looked over everyone as Ensi judged their emotional states. It was Cieras who was most likely to panic and make a misstep.

"Have Garon calm her, Ensi."

In a moment, the envoy was calmer both in appearance and in her mind. Meanwhile, Iroshi tried to think what to do. She was sure that Dukane was close by. He would want to see the results of his planning with his own eyes. Or the results of any attempts she made to resolve the situation in her favor. Most of her actions he could see through the eyes of his pets, of course, but he would want to be present. Whether she won or lost, he wanted to see with his own eyes, hear with his own ears, know every sound and smell.

What were her advantages other than knowing he was in the neighborhood? That in itself bought her very little.

Again she scanned the room, its contents and its occupants. Her gaze came to rest on Logan. One very clear advantage was that Dukane did not know that Logan was telepathic. And Logan was very good at shielding himself.

"Ensi, see if you can get Logan to listen to you. I want him to listen in on Dukane's instructions to the booreecki. Once he's caught the rhythm of it, and the sound of it, I want him to begin giving them conflicting orders. Confuse them. Even send incorrect messages back to Dukane if he can."

*Incorrect messages? Like what?*

"Like we're still here when we're not. Anything that might let people slip away."

*I am not sure about this. You know what effect the minds of the booreecki had on us. It will have the same effect on him.*

"Prepare him. Give him a taste of what they are like. How primitive they are. How bloodthirsty. Whatever you think will help."

*Why him? Why not one of us?*

"Because Dukane does not know he is telepathic."

*And what if he realizes that he is through this action?*

"Then we may very well be doomed."

He left, and she erected her own mental barrier. Logan's eyes widened, and he looked from the animals to her. He grimaced. Must have been when Ensi showed him what their minds were like. She turned her attention to the others. How long could everyone maintain an outward calm?

Cieras, of course, would be calm for quite some time. Garon had activated the endorphins produced in her own body, enough to give her a real high as if she had taken a large dose of drugs.

Everyone else relied on their own willpower and stamina. It was very difficult for them, because they had no idea who threatened them or why. In spite of the deaths of

Layton and Nole, this attack was unexpected and more frightening because of that.

Dammit! There must be some way to fight Dukane but, no matter what they did, if he detected any activity he could press that button and kill them all.

"Ensi!" Silence. He was still concentrating on Logan. "Ensi!" she called again.

*I am nearly finished.*

"Hold on a minute," she said. "The booreecki. They've been trained to shield their thoughts so they don't transmit to humans, right?"

*Yes, most of them have been. But these two . . .*

"If Logan told them what Dukane has planned, about the bomb, wouldn't they do anything they could to protect themselves?"

Ensi thought a moment.

*Yes. Especially if they are a mated pair.*

"Tell Logan."

Ensi disappeared again. The booreecki still crouched under the table, unmoving, situated so that between them they could watch the whole room. Why hadn't Dukane sent any other message? This waiting game had to be very difficult for his messengers, and they might get out of hand.

*Logan approached them,* Ensi reported. *I assisted him. They are a mated pair. The female, however, adores Dukane and will not believe he would endanger her life. The male is jealous and despises him. There is also much evidence of mistreatment.*

"None of that got back to Dukane?"

*I cannot tell for sure. I believe not. He still does not know about Logan.*

Suddenly, the male booreecky growled and seemed to turn on his mate. As Iroshi watched, it was clear, however, that he was attacking the harness that attached the bomb to her back. He got a good grip on it in his mouth and started dragging her toward the rear of the room. That was not part of Iroshi's plan.

A roar of rage filled her head. She had forgotten the barrier.

"Run!" she shouted, and turned toward the door.

She was knocked to the floor. Something heavy fell on top of her. Another roar, louder. The concussion beat at her. Everything went black.

Dukane beat his fist on the steering wheel of the car. Damn them. They could have lasted longer. If only they had taken their time. But no. They had to mess with his pets, try to turn them against him. Dukane pressed the pad.

The concussion rocked the car. Down the street, smoke and dust crashed through windows of the conference building. Windows in nearby buildings were blown in. Two people walking along the street screamed and tried to cover up as debris was blown into the street. They were knocked to the pavement and lay still.

Silently, he watched smoke, dust, and debris rise into the air, then fall back to ground. In moments, only the echo of the blast could be heard. He started the engine and raced ahead, dodging building stones and other large pieces of debris. In front of the conference hall he stopped, cut the engine, and jumped out. Dead or alive, Iroshi's body must disappear, adding to the mystery of her death. For she would be dead before the day was over.

He raced up the steps two at a time. At the doorway he stopped and peered into the foyer, then drew his sword. No use in taking any chances. He stepped over the remains of the double doors. Inside, the bodies of two of the guards lay partially buried under rubble. The other two were nowhere in sight. No one living stood in his way, and he crossed the foyer quickly. Glass and broken stone crunched under his feet. He coughed as he moved through still-settling dust.

In the weak light coming through gaps in the walls and the ruined doorway, the conference room was a shambles, but not as thoroughly destroyed as he expected. He stood just inside the doorway, hands on hips, surveying the damage. Vieren and Sandoval should be near the center of the room, the table blown clear of them. Then he spotted a piece of the tabletop and knew why. He had not seen the table, not even through his pets' eyes. It had been constructed of kiersa wood, from trees grown on—he forgot the name of the planet. It was used for such tables because of its sound-absorbing properties. Apparently, it could also absorb the effects of explosives.

No sign of the booreecki. It would have been nice to take at least one of them back with him, but there was a more important search to be made. Dukane closed his eyes and pictured the room. She had been sitting at the near side of the table with her back to the door. Very careless, although facing the door would have been useless under the circumstances.

"Is she alive?" he asked Paige. "I can't feel her."

*Yes, she is alive. Not badly hurt. But unconscious, I believe, with a concussion. Please hurry. Others will be here soon.*

"Don't lose your nerve. We're almost there. Tell me where she is."

*Ahead and to your left. Hurry.*

Dukane moved in the direction given, careful not to step on the object of his search. Suddenly he saw a flash of blue among the greys and browns. Going to his knees, he started brushing debris and dust out of the way with his gloved hands, only to find Logan lying there, dead to all appearances, although he detected a trace of life in the body. Under Logan lay Iroshi. The young man had shielded her with his own body. How gallant. How useless.

He pushed the one body aside so he could get at the

other. He felt her carotid pulse, confirming what his other senses now told him: she was alive. He rolled her over onto her back, then lifted her in his arms. Heavier than he had thought she would be. Still well muscled in spite of her slimness. Swiftly now, he made his way out of the room into the foyer. At the door he checked the street. No one had appeared yet. Surely word had gotten out by now.

He almost shrugged, but his burden prevented his doing so. With one last look, he left the building and headed for the car. Gently he deposited Iroshi in the back seat, then quickly tied her hands and feet together with the binding straps he had brought. He covered her up with a shawl he had taken from his room at the temple.

In another moment he had the car started and was moving away. In the distance, sirens at last sounded.

# 19

✦✦

Erik. Wake up. *Erik.*

The voice sounded in his head. Nearby, footsteps crunched. He knew they were footsteps, but why did they crunch? Blackness, blessed sleep, began to descend over him again, but the voice returned.

*Erik, you cannot sleep now. You must wake up. He is taking Iroshi.*

"Who's taking Iroshi?"

*Dukane. He has her in his arms and he is leaving the building.*

"Why doesn't she do something?"

He tried to find his right arm, but most of his body and limbs seemed to be very numb. Without his right arm he could not push himself up off the ground.

*She is unconscious, dammit!*

Now there was a rarity: Garon cursing. He never cursed. Ah, there was his arm, but it seemed terribly heavy. No, something was lying on it. Lots of something. Oh, it hurt to move it. He tried turning his head, but his neck hurt too much.

Damn! Dukane has Iroshi?

He pushed upright, things falling away from him as he did. Lord, he ached. Every movement was painful. And his ears rang. As he tried to push to his feet, he fell back on his rear end. His senses reeled.

*Hurry, or he will get away.*

This time, Erik knew who "he" was and why he was trying to get away. He pushed to his feet again and staggered toward the door. His sword belt was twisted, and the hilt banged against the frame as he moved through. Automatically, he straightened it on his back as he stumbled toward the outside door, then drew the sword. Even under the grey, swirling sky, the light was too bright, and he shaded his eyes. Down the street a large car sped away.

*Too late,* Garon said.

"That was him, I guess."

*Yes, that was him. Iroshi is in the back seat.*

"Can you trace him?"

*I could for a while. He had his barrier down while he searched for her.*

"Why didn't you try to stop him somehow?"

Sirens sounded in the distance. At least the city was waking up to the disaster.

*I was pretty dazed too. Once he found her, he raised the barrier.*

"Any idea where he plans to take her?"

*None.*

"What about Ensi? Shouldn't he be in touch?" He turned toward the conference room doorway.

*If she is unconscious, he may be too. Perhaps Dukane has some way of shielding both of them from us. I do not know.*

In the conference room, there was no movement, no sound. Even falling dust had stopped. Slightly to the left, a blue patch stood out, and he went to see if it was Logan. It was the Athenian, lying on his back, which seemed odd, since everyone should be lying on their stomachs if they had turned to run. Then he remembered. Logan had pushed Iroshi to the floor just as the bomb went off. She must have been under him, and Dukane had to roll him to one side to get at her.

The young man's pulse was weak but he was alive.

"See if you can help him, Garon."

The companion complied without a word. Erik started to look for any particular wound that needed tending. Just then, a loud commotion rose in the foyer. He tensed a moment, remembering the earlier commotion, but this time it was the rescue crews, arrived at last. Someone gave orders out there; then a small bunch of people came into the conference room.

"Damn!" one of them said.

The same voice began giving orders again. People scurried around. A medic came to Erik and led him to one side by his uninjured arm. She splintered his arm then began tending to his cuts and bruises, most of them on his face, neck, and hands, which had been exposed. One cut on his scalp was particularly tender, and he flinched as she applied antiseptic. Before she was done with him, lights had been set up for the workers and more people had been uncovered.

Cieras came to a few moments after being freed. A string of invectives followed her release, which meant that she was not hurt badly. Yenson soon had his broken arm in a sling. One of his guards was dead, as was one of Cieras's staff. Logan had suffered a particularly bad blow on the head and a couple of broken ribs. There might also be some internal injuries, but the medic was not sure. He was the first taken to the hospital.

*I will check on him periodically,* Garon said as he returned to Erik.

"Will he live?"

*I do not know.*

Yenson approached, his face pale and his jaw set.

"I understand Iroshi is not here," he said. He winced as he sat on the bench next to Erik.

"No. Dukane took her."

"She was alive?" Erik nodded. "You didn't stop him?"

"I was nearly unconscious. I tried, but he was too fast."

"Any idea where?"

"None. Wherever he's been hiding for the last day or so, I would imagine."

Yenson glanced at him sideways. "Do you think he will kill her?"

"Yes, I do. And I don't think he will wait very long."

The car turned another corner, and Iroshi tried to keep the motion from rocking her onto the scabbard still slung across her back. She had been placed on her back, and the damn thing dug in every time she put any weight on it. If she could stay propped against the back of the seat, that would also put less pressure on her arms bound behind her.

More disturbing was not being able to raise Ensi. Such concussions could render companions unconscious, too, but they usually roused much more quickly than did their hosts. So far, no sign of his presence. He had to contact Erik and Garon to let them know where they were being taken. Assuming he had some idea.

The car must have entered some sort of tunnel or garage from the echoes. Tunnel more likely, because they drove on quite a ways before stopping. The sound of the engine still echoed back off walls that were rather close on each side.

Dukane cut the engine and got out. He slammed the front door shut and opened the back door. As he lifted Iroshi to a sitting position, he carefully adjusted the shawl around her, keeping her from seeing where they were. As much a gesture of intimidation as one of practicality.

"No use in calling out," he said. "People rarely come down here."

He got a shoulder under her and lifted. Slung across him like that, and with the jouncing as he walked away, she could hardly have called out anyway. Breathing was difficult enough.

Dukane opened and closed three doors before he finally put her down. She lay there, trying to catch her breath as she heard him move around what sounded like a rather large room. Weak light filtered through the shawl, but she could see nothing more than that.

"Ensi, where are you?"

Could he have been seriously harmed by the explosion? Nothing like that had been experienced before.

*I am here, Iroshi,* he said at last.

"Where have you been?"

*Like you, I was unconscious for a time.*

"And then?"

*I have been talking with Paige. Or, rather, she has been talking to me. Telling me the rules, as it were.*

"Rules? You told Garon where we are, didn't you? The hell with any rules."

*The rules prevent my doing so.*

"All right. I suppose I need to know these rules, too."

*Yes. I am not allowed to communicate with anyone outside this room. Paige will be monitoring me at every moment.*

"Therefore, you can't tell anyone where we are."

*Right.*

"Do you know where we are?"

*Not exactly. I have a good idea, though.*

"Back to the rules."

*If I attempt to contact Garon or anyone else, another bomb will be set off in Dr. Drace's laboratory. If that happens, there is a good chance that everything having to do with the formula, including Dr. Drace's assistants, will be destroyed. Another bomb has been placed in the Pritchard Sanitarium where Mrs. Nole is again a patient. A third bomb is in this very room.*

"He'd rather we both died than for me to get away, huh?"

*Exactly.*

"Is Paige monitoring us right now?"

*Only to make sure I don't go beyond these walls. She has given us a few minutes to talk first.*

"What kind of a mood is she in? Does she go along with the things that Dukane is doing?"

*I think not. She . . . is returning.*

Ensi faded away, and the only sound Iroshi had was that of Dukane doing something else in the room. She shifted position, trying to keep the scabbard from digging into her shoulder.

"Lie still," Dukane ordered.

"I'm uncomfortable," she said. "Surely you can untie me now."

"In a moment. I've a few last-minute things to do."

Gods, if only she was a true telepath instead of a sensitive. If Paige was watching over Ensi, she might be able to communicate to Garon herself. Or was Dukane monitoring her? Too late, they had found out that he could do that sort of thing.

Suddenly, the noises stopped and she could feel Dukane walking toward her. He unwound the shawl from around her and bent to undo the straps from her ankles. The light hurt her eyes and she blinked. For only a moment, she could see the room but could not quite take it all in before he stepped in close to undo her wrists. Her cheek pressed against his belly as he leaned over. Her wrists freed, he grabbed the sword scabbard and lifted the belt over her head. He carried it to the far side of the room, propping it against the wall, giving her a chance, at last, to get a good look over at her surroundings.

The first thing she noticed was that there were no windows. She sat on a chaise lounge that was covered in rich red velvet. It was set near the wall at one end of the room. At the other end was a strange combination of furnishings. A wooden altar sat in the center about six feet from the wall. Against the wall behind that was a wooden bench. On either side sat braziers that contained some burning substance. Smoke swirled upward but did not fill the air. An invisible air circulation system must draw it out, leaving the air fresh. She suspected that much of the noise she heard after they first arrived was Dukane getting the braziers lit.

He stood off to the right, watching her reaction to his preparations. Considering there was little else in the room, they were minimal.

She stood, and a pain in her right leg made her gasp. At least a bruise in her thigh or, at worst, a pulled tendon or ligament. Her left wrist hurt and was swelling. Dukane's sword scabbard was propped against the wall, along with her own, just to his left. Nothing else that could be used as a weapon was in sight.

"Well, what do you think?" he asked.

"About what?"

"The room, of course."

"What is it for?"

"For you. This is where you will become a goddess."

"And how will I do that?"

He grinned. "You know how."

"What if I don't want to die in order to become a goddess? What if I don't want to become a goddess at all?"

"That's what all of this is about, isn't it? To save you from yourself. You must not waste the image you have built nor the adoration of so many people."

"Adoration?" She limped to the altar. It was old and worn, and she could imagine her body lying across it, her throat cut, dying so that some stupid religion could be born. "I don't want adoration. I want to die as I lived. With a sword in my hand, fighting to the death."

"Is that a challenge?"

She laughed. "Yes, I suppose it was. If I'd thought about it, though, I would never have said that. You wouldn't fight me fairly, if at all."

She left the altar and started toward him. The door opened, and two of Dukane's followers entered, a man and a woman. They closed the door and stopped just inside the room.

"Nice try, my dear, but you're right. I won't fight you. I assume Ensi has told you about the bombs." She nodded. He pulled a control box from the pocket of his cloak. "I will set them off if you try to escape."

He motioned to the two newcomers and they approached her. The man took hold of her jacket by the lapels and started to take it off. Iroshi shrugged him away.

"Cline and Wessell are going to dress you for the ceremony," Dukane said, pointing alternately at the man and the woman. "Please don't make this more difficult than it has to be."

The woman had laid out a gorgeous robe of silver lamé on the lounge. It was designed identically to the robes worn by new members of the Glaive on their initiation, except for the cloth from which it was made. She helped the man take off the grey uniform, her boots, and underclothes. Finally, Iroshi stood naked. Wessell took the pins from her hair and let it cascade down her back. Dukane looked at her with eyes that could have devoured her.

"Stop," he ordered and the two stood still. Iroshi wanted to squirm under his gaze, but managed not to.

"You are still a very beautiful woman," he said with awe.

He signaled the two underlings to continue, and they helped her get the robe on. They fastened it down the front and arranged the hem around her on the floor. The thing was heavier than it looked, and for a moment she hoped that she would not have to wear it very long. On the other hand, it might be better to wear it as long as possible. At another signal from Dukane, they left as silently as they had entered.

"How do you intend killing me?" Iroshi asked.

"I hope to convince you to kill yourself." She looked up at that, unable to believe what he said. "Barring that, I will use one of the swords. Your own, perhaps. Or the Great Pallasch. I may even do it from within."

He insinuated himself into her mind, gripping her, squeezing the breath out of her. She had been unprepared, and Ensi was not there. Dukane squeezed and she gasped for air. Her knees were about to give way when he stopped.

"How easy it would be," he said.

"There's no challenge in that," she gasped. "No glory."

"I'm not looking for glory in your actual death," he said, and his voice had turned hateful. "I intend for you to disappear. You died already as far as anyone knows, although they will never know exactly how you died. Everyone will believe that you must have died in the explosion and that your body was either totally obliterated, or it was mysteriously transported elsewhere. People love mystery religions. By the same token, many in the Glaive will live in hope of your eventual return, either in body or spirit."

He walked to the altar and stood behind it. His hands caressed the top. Slowly, she erected the barriers in her mind.

"Don't think for one minute of going into revay. That is just another form of escape that will cause the deaths of so many individuals."

"What of Ensi? What do you plan for him?"

"I don't think I could trust him any more than I can trust you. He shall die with you, I think."

They both could not die. So much knowledge, so much experience, would be lost to the Glaive if that happened. Was preserving those two qualities for the future worth the deaths of a dozen—a hundred—people? Or was she fooling herself? No one was irreplaceable, after all. Were they?

"I'm sure neither of you would risk so many lives to save yourself," Dukane was saying. "You're too honorable and care too much."

So, he didn't even guess how ruthless they could be. A side they had managed to camouflage from one of their own. But then the stakes had never been quite so high before. There must be no doubt in her own mind: she would sacrifice anything, any number of people for the Glaive. Ensi may not be as willing as she was, though.

Dukane had come to the end of his ramblings.

"When am I to die?" she asked.

"Ah, Iroshi of the Glaive is in a hurry?"

"Not really."

He smiled. "Soon. Very soon." The smile disappeared. "Truth to tell, I find myself somewhat reluctant to be in a hurry. Except for that last visit on Rune-Nelson, we haven't had a real conversation in a very long time. Even that last time, we didn't talk long."

"No, we didn't."

"However, we can't really prolong this, can we?"

She chuckled. "Clearly, I don't share your eagerness."

He came around the altar. "You would if you could just understand." His voice turned earnest. "What I'm doing is giving you true immortality, even greater than you could possibly hope for as a companion of the Glaive. You will be adored by all following generations."

"But I won't be able to enjoy it, will I? I would prefer to achieve immortality by not dying."

*Iroshi, Paige is weakening in her resolve.*

"Keep at her. She is our weak link." Aloud she asked, "What about your two followers? They know I didn't die in the explosion."

"They won't tell anyone. I'll make sure of that."

"You're going to kill them, too?"

That he would contemplate such a thing was not surprising. Letting him think that the idea was abhorrent to her might buy her—or them—something, if only a little time.

"Not if I don't have to," Dukane said.

Iroshi let out a big sigh. "Dammit, Dukane, it doesn't have to end this way. Enough people have died. Isn't there some compromise we can reach?"

"You see," he said, pointing at her. "You are growing weak. You must go before you ruin your whole image. You're losing the edge that made you great. Although I have to admit that the way you set up Pryhs and Layton was very clever, you are losing that edge. You're getting older and have less of the old fire."

She laughed out loud. "I'm only eighty-seven."

"Oh, I didn't say you were old," he said quickly. He came to sit beside her on the chaise and took her right hand in both of his. "But, at your age, things can only go downhill."

Her sword wiggled slightly and started to withdraw from the scabbard. Iroshi turned, trying to maneuver Dukane around so that he could not see the movement out of the corner of his eye.

"Maybe, with your guidance, I can keep that from happening," she said, trying to sound as if the thought of growing old and impotent filled her with dread. "I didn't understand before. I'm not sure I do now . . ."

He threw her hand away and jumped to his feet. "Don't try to toy with me, Iroshi!" he shouted. "I'm not some enamored young man you can wrap around your finger."

The katana came free of its scabbard and hung suspended near the wall. *Hurry, Ensi,* she thought. She pressed the vision down, afraid that Dukane might see it in her mind. But not quickly enough. Dukane whirled, saw the katana, and leapt for it. She could almost hear him shouting for Paige.

He fumbled in his pocket for the control box, and it fell from his fingers to the floor. Ensi had to have done that, too. The man shouted, while the companion was silent. Why didn't Ensi say something?

The sword swooped over Dukane's head toward her. The pommel nearly smacked her in the temple, but she managed to grab the grip in time. The weapon resisted her control a moment; then its full weight rested in her hand. Meanwhile, Dukane, torn between lunging for the control box or his own sword, hesitated a moment too long. The box skittered across the floor, coming to rest against the altar. The sword now nearer his hand, Dukane grabbed it up, glancing at the box before turning to face Iroshi.

The katana felt good in her hands. Its voices spoke to her along the nerves of her fingers, up through her arms. Familiar voices that cried of honor, combat, and death. She was not afraid. She had faced this enemy before and would have bested him then if not for a stupid trick. However, instead of closing in, Dukane shouted. The door opened and his two followers came back into the room. The woman was armed with a naginata, the pole taller than she was herself and the shining blade long and plain. The man carried an elegantly made cavalry saber, although it too was plain.

"Get the control box," Dukane ordered.

Iroshi whirled the katana in a ritual pattern and danced across the room. Dukane started to head her off. Wessell started around the man but stopped when the box rose in the air and wobbled behind the altar.

"Paige!" Dukane shouted. "Stop him."

At that moment, Iroshi realized that it wasn't Ensi who had moved the box.

# 20

✦✦

"You found her?" Erik asked.

*More or less. Ensi made momentary contact, and I followed his trail back. I still don't know exactly where she is, but I am sure it is in or near the temple.*

"Can you maintain contact?"

*It is too dangerous. Dukane has threatened to kill a number of people if she or Ensi tried to escape or to contact us.*

He went on to explain about bombs placed in various locations around the city and that Dukane planned to kill Iroshi, and very soon. Ensi's immediate problem was Paige's monitoring his and Iroshi's thoughts. Ensi was working on the companion's sense of loyalty and had managed to slip through for a moment, but had been unable to impart any further information.

"It's not enough, but under the circumstances, I'm surprised he managed so much," Erik said. "We'll have to contact Yenson about the bombs. Maybe his people can ferret them out before Dukane feels that he is forced to set them off."

The major's arm had been set and he had accepted something for that pain and a king-sized headache. He had already set elements of the guards to the task of trying to find Iroshi and Dukane. No one had much hope for success in that area, but the effort had to be made.

*I doubt that we will have enough time to find them,*

Garon said, referring to the bombs. *One of them is there with Iroshi.*

"Oh," Erik said and paused. "We have no choice. There are also a limited number of places he could set the rest to have the maximum effect he wants: the palace, the temple maybe where they are. We might get lucky. I'm worried about Iroshi, though. I don't know how we can help her."

They both fell silent. Erik started pacing again. In the next room, drifting in and out of consciousness, Logan fought to live. Erik and his companion had decided to work from the hospital so they could help Iroshi's new friend as much as possible. They had come to like him, but felt they owed him a debt of gratitude, since his injuries were, in part, a result of his attempt to save Iroshi from the worst effects of the blast. The young man was in danger of losing his life, and they had to do everything they could to bolster his chances for survival.

Erik sat down in a chair. Next to him a comm unit monitored the communications of Yenson's forces. Around the room, other equipment worked to keep Erik in touch and at hand. He needed all of it because Garon was kept busy helping Logan and listening for Ensi.

The one he wanted most to be in touch with was Iroshi. This was one of the few times he could not help feeling that she was not going to extricate herself from the danger she found herself in.

"Wait a minute," he said to Garon. "Paige and Dukane are aware of us and Iroshi and Ensi. It's possible he brought some of his followers from the Glaive, and they are also aware of them."

*Yes. That is why we do not dare try to make contact.*

Garon was aware, of course, that he was restating what was already known. However, there was a factor only Iroshi had thought of.

"They are not aware of Logan, are they?"

*No, but he is unable to do anything.*

"That isn't entirely true."

*Yes, it is.*

"No, Garon. With our help, he could reach out to Iroshi. You could lead him along the path you followed before. Between the two of us, we could prop him up, give him the additional strength he needs to find and help her."

*He is near death. He needs to use all of his strength and concentration on surviving.*

"I am sure he would do anything to help Iroshi."

*It would not be fair to ask such a thing of him.*

"Ask him, Garon."

*Iroshi would not approve of his sacrificing himself for her.*

"She has always said that we should do whatever is necessary to ensure the survival of the Glaive. This is truly one time when her survival is the key to our survival as a guild. Ask him."

Garon disappeared without another word. Erik rested his elbows on his knees and rubbed his burning eyes. His whole body felt like it had been days since he last slept. The cracked ribs ached constantly, and the bindings around them were so tight it was difficult to breathe. His arm, now in a sling, ached constantly. His ears still rang. And he wished nothing more than for Iroshi to appear and tell him he was doing the right thing. Or, better still, to take the decision on herself. She was good at that. Always willing to do whatever was necessary to protect the client and the Glaive, not necessarily in that order.

Even if she disapproved of his decision, he could not do otherwise. If Dukane won this battle, he pretty much won the war, even if he himself did not survive. His followers would keep the banner raised, and before anyone could stop it, the Iroshi cult would win out. Even if it did not take over the whole of the Glaive, it would splinter the guild, destroying its effectiveness and giving it problems that it could not survive.

Erik felt Garon return. It was a moment before he spoke.

*I have asked him,* Garon said. *He will do it.*

"He knows the risks?"

*Yes.*

"Can he remain conscious enough to do it?"

*With our help.*

"Let's go, then."

Garon brought the other two together. Erik almost changed his mind when he felt how weak Logan was. They had to prop him up between them as Garon led the way. The Athenian had never projected himself in this way before. Even Erik got light-headed, and Garon coached and prodded the two as scenes and time flashed past.

They stopped, and the two Glaivers quickly pressed behind Logan. Paige would not be looking for him, and if they could keep their own presences hidden, they just might get away with this.

In a windowless room, Dukane sat on a chaise beside Iroshi, her hand in his. They talked, but the words were distorted.

"Her sword," Erik said, as he spied it leaning against one of the walls. "He has his back to it. Can we get it to her?"

*We must first find the detonation control box,* Garon pointed out.

Logan reached out and touched Dukane's mind. "It's in his pocket," he said after several moments.

"Let's work on the sword, then. If Iroshi keeps his attention, we can try to get it to her. While he's distracted by that, we'll go for the box."

Everyone agreed. Using Logan's skills, Garon guided the young man, teaching him to grasp the hilt of the sword. It wiggled as he tried to draw it from the scabbard. His strength was not quite up to it, and the others added theirs to his. Once, they had to stop as Paige flashed past.

Suddenly Dukane jumped to his feet, his face flushed. With one last mighty effort, the katana came free. Dukane whirled, saw the sword, and leapt for it. They lifted it over his head, nearly hit Iroshi in the head with the pommel, but she grabbed the hilt and held on.

They released the sword to her, then turned their attention to the box. Logan's remaining strength was fading quickly. They grabbed at the box as Dukane pulled it from his pocket, but could not hold on as Dukane fumbled for it at the same time. It fell to the floor. Logan pushed it across the floor. When two of Dukane's followers entered the room and made for the box, he flipped it behind the altar with one final effort.

"Ensi!" Iroshi called.

The three opponents circled her. Dukane clearly had his mind on the control box as much as on her.

*I am here.*

"Get control of the box."

*I have.*

"But you didn't . . ."

*No, it was Logan with Erik and Garon.*

"They're all right, then."

Filled with a sense of relief, she turned to keep Dukane directly in front of her. The other two would not attack without his direction. At the same time, she tried to maneuver herself closer to one of the walls.

*I will keep Paige out of the fight,* Ensi said. *Garon will try to get the attention of the other two.*

All right. He had ignored her statement about "they" being all right. That meant that either Erik or Logan was injured. That was a worry for later. At the moment, she had three skilled warriors to face, all of them younger than her and single-minded. Such a strange thing: they were willing to kill the person they wished to worship because of their devotion to another. Dukane's wish to kill her she understood. Their willingness could only come from their devotion to him.

Cline stepped in toward her and just as quickly stepped back. Iroshi pretended to be distracted by his feint and Dukane swung his sword in an overhand arc. She parried easily and pushed his blade aside. Wessell lunged with the naginata. Iroshi whirled, got tangled in the hem of the robe, but struck the blade aside. She regained her balance and struck at the man, who barely raised his own blade in time.

Her injured leg gave way slightly and she faltered a moment. The pain lessened and she stood ready, once more facing Dukane. He smiled. He had seen the pain and the weakness.

"Stand back," he told his two followers. "I can handle this."

They moved away, their confidence in their leader so complete that they uttered no protest. Dukane bowed to Iroshi, the smile still on his face.

"You will be immortal in spite of yourself," he said.

He attacked in the traditional kendo style: right foot leading, pounding the floor as it pulled him forward. The Great Pallasch was so much longer than her katana. Although she met each blow successfully, her weak leg and shorter blade made it difficult to defend. They stood facing each other again; then she attacked in the same manner.

The red haze began. With each stroke of the sword, it grew. The pain in her leg became part of her entire body, her mind. Dukane countered and she knew his blade had slipped in, cutting her right side. That pain jolted the other. She felt the impact of the swords coming together, gloried in their strength and the ring of their metal.

The void descended. The sound of Dukane's breathing

and kiai stretched and distorted along with her own. Energy flowed from her to the swords and back. He had not entered the void, and she wondered vaguely if he could. He was once able to do so, she knew that, although not as readily as she did. Perhaps his new religion had taken away from the depth of his devotion to the sword. Or perhaps the manner in which he had chosen the sword kept the weapon from being entirely his.

They attacked and defended. The weight of the robe, the pain of her wounds, sapped her strength. She was growing tired but did not yet feel the impact of fatigue. Her next attack forced Dukane back. He was weakening even more than she was. He was beginning to be afraid. Back and back she pushed him.

"Get her!" he called to his followers.

They rushed from behind but she turned on them. One blow with the katana sliced through the wooden pole of the naginata, breaking it in two. Its blade clanged to the floor. She attacked the man, forcing him back against the altar. She pushed his blade down and brought her own up, slicing him across the abdomen. The woman had recovered and picked up the shortened end of the pole with the blade attached.

*Behind you!* Ensi cried.

Iroshi turned. Dukane raced toward her with his sword upraised. She went down on one knee and thrust forward. The tip of the katana pierced his abdomen. He staggered forward, pushing her blade farther in. His own crashed down, and she just barely slipped aside in time. She pressed the katana, pushing him back at the same time.

The woman behind her screamed. Iroshi picked up Dukane's sword by the blade and thrust behind her. The blade of the naginata brushed her shoulder and she crumpled to the floor.

The fight was over, win or lose, and the void faded. All

the pain came through. Her leg. Her side. Her shoulder. Even her fear, both for herself and an as yet unnamed friend who was sorely wounded.

The floor felt cool against her cheek as she turned onto her side. She was more tired than she had ever been before in her life. Her eyes closed. Ensi called, but he would have to wait. She needed rest. From everything.

Eventually, she pushed herself erect. Her hands hurt, and she looked down. Blood smeared across the floor where she had pressed them against the stone. The blade of Dukane's sword had sliced each hand when she grabbed it: across the four fingers.

She staggered to her feet and grasped the handle of the long sword to pull it free. Wessell's body did not move. She held the weapon in her hands, her blood adding to the voices in its blade, a feeling of relief coming over her that it would no longer be used by a dishonored man. Those voices told her that the relief was not hers alone.

Iroshi moved toward Dukane to do the same with her katana. When it came free, his body jerked spasmodically. She tried to lift the sword, to be ready to defend, but her body could not summon the strength. His body stopped moving. She placed the point of her sword on the floor and leaned on it, watching Dukane. She should probably check to make sure he was dead. She was just too tired.

What was Ensi doing? Probably contacting Garon and Erik to let them know where she was.

She staggered to the chaise and sat down. Very carefully, she raised both swords to lay them beside her. It would be nice to lie down, but she did not have the strength to raise her feet.

Something slammed into her mind, grasping and clawing at her. Iroshi raised both fists to her temples, tensing, trying to protect against the assault. Paige thrashed around, hitting here and there, blinded by her own pain and sense of loss.

"Ensi!" Iroshi cried.

She pushed at the other companion, trying to force her back. Ensi appeared and grappled at Paige. Iroshi placed her arms over her head, trying to hold in what sanity remained. Trying to keep her head from bursting.

*We killed Logan. Now I will kill you,* Paige screamed.

A sense of loss overwhelmed Iroshi, and she collapsed onto the chaise, her feet dangling to the floor. Ensi got hold of Paige at last; then Garon appeared. Between the two of them, they got control of the renegade companion. All three disappeared, and Iroshi drifted into unconsciousness.

*Iroshi, I am here,* Ensi said softly a few minutes later. *The others are coming for you.*

"I'll sleep now," she said, wondering if this part was a dream.

# 21

✧

Logan lay very still, his face pale, his breathing shallow. The doctors would not say what his chances for survival were. He had taken a sudden turn for the worse, they said, which they could not explain. The timing had coincided with his struggle to save Iroshi, of course.

Two days had passed since she won her freedom, and Iroshi was still tired. The first night, she had slept as the dead sleep, after her own wounds had been taken care of. She had slept little the next night; had, in fact, maintained a vigil at Logan's bedside, asking Ensi and Garon to do more than they could and holding Logan's hand. He had risked his life for her. It was the least she could do for him.

It wasn't obligation that kept her there, although she had not admitted that to herself. She was in one of her self-recriminating moods, which she had come to recognize over the years and which occurred every time she had to do something ruthless. Or something ruthless was done in her name.

She had wanted to be angry with Erik and Garon for risking Logan's life to save her. Even wanted to be mad at Logan for agreeing. He could not be blamed, of course. He was terribly vulnerable at the time.

She released his hand, stood, and stretched. She needed another walkabout. She put on her coat, hat, and gloves. Outside the room, she stretched again. A slight smell of food made her stomach seem impossibly empty. Probably

Erik and Cieras were in the waiting room, having some snack. Or, would it be lunch or dinner? It was hours since she had eaten, and she was hungry. In a moment, she would join the two there and see what they had. Maybe she would just go to the dining hall and see if anything there appealed to her.

She turned right, toward the side entrance to the hospital. Outside, it was snowing again. White flakes fell thickly from a leaden sky, adding to the depth of white and brown snow already piled two feet deep. She pulled the coat close around her and started down the heated sidewalk. Steam rose into the air but appeared to freeze and fall back down as more snow. An optical illusion, she was sure, but an interesting sight.

Now that she was on the move, her head seemed to be clearing somewhat. Back in that too-warm room, she was having difficulty coming to terms with everything that had happened in the past forty-eight hours. Even in the crisper air, some of it was very hard to accept.

Neither Dukane's death nor Logan's endangering himself at the urging of Erik and Garon was the worst of it. The third event had been Ensi's and showed how angry the actions of Paige had made him; something she had not realized before. That a companion would, or even could, betray the Glaive was a bitter lesson for him, even though Paige was not one of the original companions.

The worst thought that crossed her mind was the possibility that Ensi may have acted out of revenge rather than necessity. No matter how much they discussed it, she could not believe that Ensi would ever act purely out of a vengeful mood. Still, there had been no remorse when he told her what had happened.

Paige had stayed very close to Ensi, ensuring that he made contact with no one outside the cell. Even so, he had managed the one short contact with Garon while she wrestled with her conscience. Just an instant, but so much could be transmitted in an instant.

When Logan had moved the sword, Ensi had immediately begun to struggle with Paige to keep her from contacting Dukane. Ensi's superior experience had been the factor that brought success. He had wrestled his adversary to the ground, so to speak, and held her there. In that position, he had been unable to help Iroshi in her fight with Dukane and his followers, even though Paige promised that she would do nothing further to assist her host if they would just promise he would not be harmed.

When Dukane died, Paige stayed behind because of that stranglehold that Ensi had on her, until he left to contact Garon. As soon as he was gone, she had attacked Iroshi, infuriated by the death of her host. On hearing Iroshi call out to him, Ensi had immediately tried to pull Paige away, but she fought like a tigress. Only with Garon's help was he able to stop her in time.

Once she was subdued, the problem remained as to what to do with the homeless companion. Merely leaving Paige to drift where she pleased was not an option; she was a danger to them all. Eventually, she would enter other people's minds on her own and become a total nuisance to the Djedians.

Then it occurred to Ensi. He knew where Mrs. Nole was. She had been taken back to the sanitarium after her wounds were treated. She had no mind to mess with, and thus would be in no danger. He called Garon and told him what he planned; they grabbed Paige up and raced to find the new host. Once the prisoner understood what was happening, she struggled desperately, but Ensi and Garon were more powerful. Between the two of them, they managed to get her bound so that she could not escape.

Ensi backed away and surveyed Paige's prison. Total emptiness with windows on the world where she could not act. A body that would no longer move. She might go mad in such a place, if she was not already mad. The companions would have to check on her every once in a while. If the future went well, maybe she would learn from her mistakes and from observing the world over the next few decades. There would be plenty of time for that. She might choose to die in her loneliness. They all had that ability, but never before had one of them been given this much reason to use it.

Ensi had displayed little emotion in the telling except for the anger. No regret, no sympathy. Just a matter-of-fact telling of necessary actions taken. Looked at rationally, it was no more, nor no less, than Iroshi would have done herself. Yet she shivered and knew it was not because of the cold, although the sun was setting and the temperature was dropping.

Back in the hospital, Logan lay fighting for his life. Miles away, in the sanitarium, Paige sat, bound, perhaps wishing she might die. Where did the companion's courage lie? In her will to learn and live, or in her desire to die rather than expend all that time and energy?

She knew where her own courage lay. Enough people had died in this cursed business, and she did not intend to let Logan be the last one. He would get better, and he would come into the Glaive. Whether he and she remained lovers was to be seen. However, he would be a welcome addition, and she wanted him to know more about her and the guild. Besides, she needed his help in finishing up the negotiations regarding persea.

She turned around and walked back toward the hospital. Snow still fell and it seemed to get darker with each step. Then lights came on over the grounds, lighting her way.

*Iroshi,* Ensi called. *Logan is waking.*

She nodded in satisfaction. Now everything would be right with the Glaive again. Until the next crisis. When it came, gods grant that she was dead and gone. She laughed silently. That was not a likely scenario in any event. Maybe, instead, she would join Paige in a lifeless body where she, too, could learn and observe without being a hazard to anyone.

Somehow, she suspected Iroshi of the Glaive would always be a hazard to someone.

# STEVE PERRY

**__THE FOREVER DRUG 0-441-00142-4/$5.50**
When Venture Silk's lover was murdered on Earth, the only thing Silk escaped with was his life. A master at deception, he must now keep enemy agents from the vital secret contained in her blood.

**__SPINDOC  0-441-00008-8/$5.50**
Venture Silk is a liar-for-hire who manipulates the public's perception. But when his lover is murdered and Silk becomes a target of assassins, he must see through the deception to find the one thing he never worried about before—the truth.

## THE MATADOR SERIES
"Inventive genius...one of our better contemporary writers."—*Science Fiction Review*

__THE MAN WHO NEVER MISSED  0-441-51918-0/$4.99
__THE MACHIAVELLI INTERFACE  0-441-51356-5/$4.99
__THE ALBINO KNIFE  0-441-01391-0/$4.99
__BROTHER DEATH  0-441-54476-2/$4.99

Payable in U.S. funds. No cash orders accepted. Postage & handling: $1.75 for one book, 75¢ for each additional. Maximum postage $5.50. Prices, postage and handling charges may change without notice. Visa, Amex, MasterCard call 1-800-788-6262, ext. 1, refer to ad # 536b

Or, check above books and send this order form to:
The Berkley Publishing Group
390 Murray Hill Pkwy., Dept. B
East Rutherford, NJ 07073

Bill my: ☐ Visa ☐ MasterCard ☐ Amex (expires)
Card#_____
($15 minimum)
Signature_____

Please allow 6 weeks for delivery.  Or enclosed is my: ☐ check ☐ money order

Name_____  Book Total $_____
Address_____  Postage & Handling $_____
City_____  Applicable Sales Tax $_____
(NY, NJ, PA, CA, GST Can.)
State/ZIP_____  Total Amount Due $_____